# 홍길동젼

셰동대왕즉위십오연의홍희문밧긔 ᄒᆞᆫ저상이
홍이오명은문이니우인이쳥염강직ᄒᆞ여덕망이거록
셰의영웅이라일직용문의올나벼살이한림의쳐ᄒᆞ
엿더니명망이됴졍의웃듬되미젼하그덕망을승이녀기ᄉᆞ
벼살을도〻와이조판서로좌의졍을ᄒᆞ이시니승상이국은을
감동ᄒᆞ야갈츙보국ᄒᆞ니ᄉᆞ방의일이업고도젹이업스미시
화연풍ᄒᆞ여나라이틱평ᄒᆞ더라일〻은승상난간의비겨잠ᄀᆞᆫ
조의더니ᄒᆞᆫ풍이길을인도ᄒᆞ여ᄒᆞᆫ고듸다〻르니쳥산은암
암ᄒᆞ고녹슈난양〻ᄒᆞᆫ듸셰류쳔만가지녹음이파ᄉᆞᄒᆞ고황
금갓튼꾀ᄭᅩ리난츈흥을희롱ᄒᆞ여냥뉴간의왕니ᄒᆞ며기화
요초만발ᄒᆞᆫ듸쳥학빅학이며비취공작이츈광을ᄌᆞ랑ᄒᆞ
거날승상이경물을구경ᄒᆞ며졈〻드러가니만장졀벽은하
날의다엇고구비〻〻벽계슈난골〻이폭포되어오운이어려
엿난듸길이쓴쳐갈바을모로더니문득쳥룡이물결을헤

치고머리을드러고함ᄒᆞ니산학이문허지난듯ᄒᆞ더니그용
이입을버리고긔운을토ᄒᆞ여승상의입으로드러뵈거날ᄭᆡ
다르니평싱디몽이라니염의혜아리되필련군ᄌᆞ을나흐리라
ᄒᆞ여즉시니당의드러가시비을물이치고부인을익그러취침
코져ᄒᆞ니부인이졍식왈승상은국지저상이라체위존즁ᄒᆞ
시거날빅쥬의졍실의드러와노류장화갓치ᄒᆞ시니저상의
체면이어듸잇나잇가승상이싱각ᄒᆞ신즉말ᄉᆞᆷ은당연ᄒᆞ오

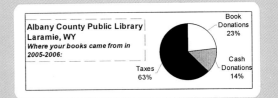

# The Legend of Hong Kil Dong

## THE ROBIN HOOD OF KOREA

Anne Sibley O'Brien

Charlesbridge

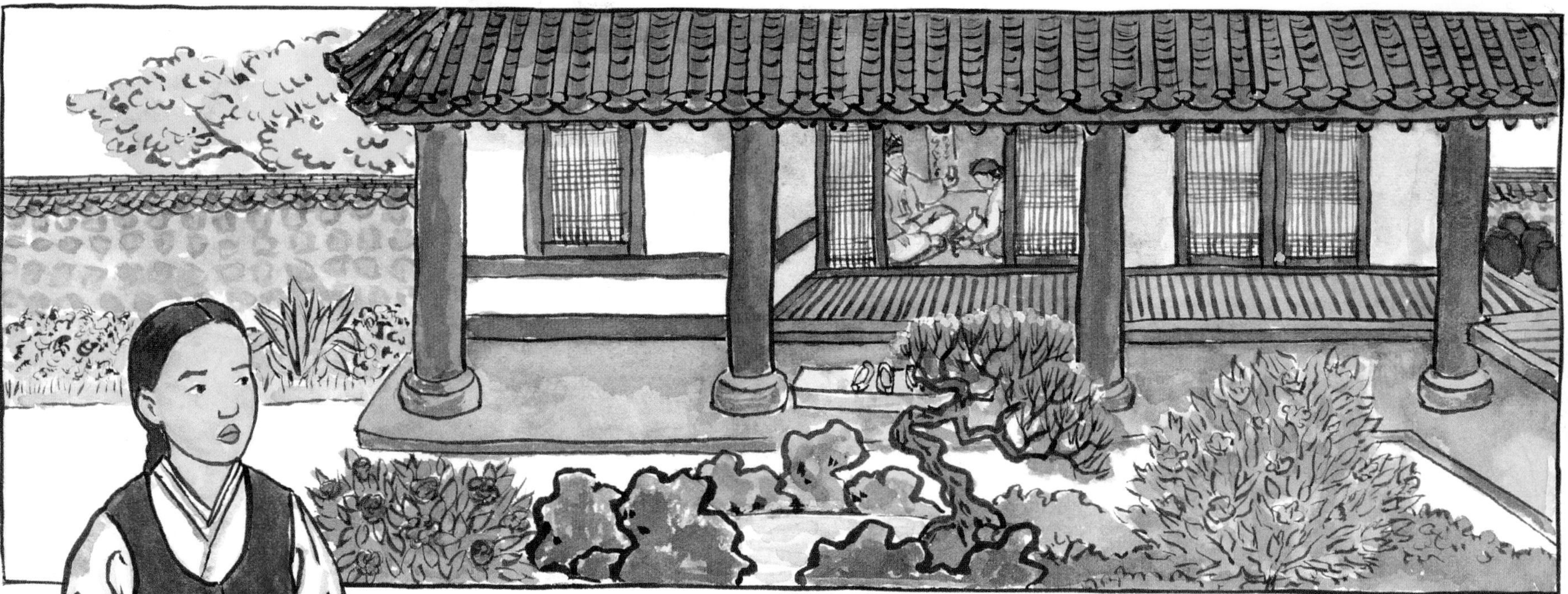

I CHING HEXAGRAM AND INTERPRETATION:
FOLLOWING/PURSUIT: NEED FOR FLEXIBILITY AND ADAPTABILITY

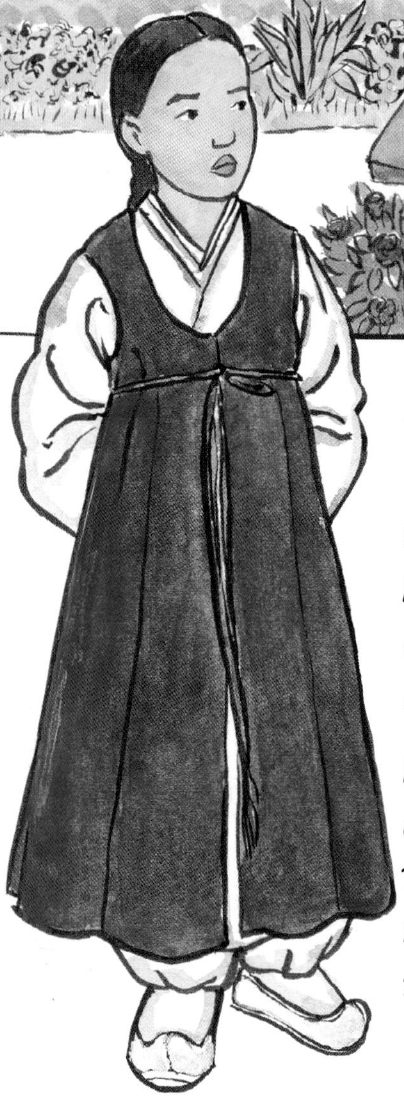

# The story begins this way...

Once there was a boy who could not claim his father. KIL DONG, as he was called, was the second son of a wealthy and powerful advisor to the king, Minister HONG.

But KIL DONG's mother was not the noble wife of the minister. She was only a maidservant. Though raised as a son in the same household, KIL DONG was not allowed to call the minister "father."

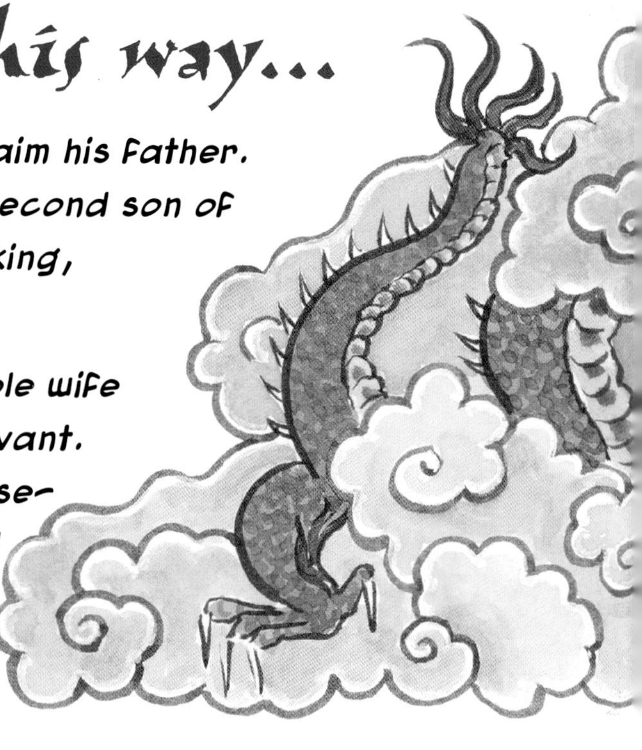

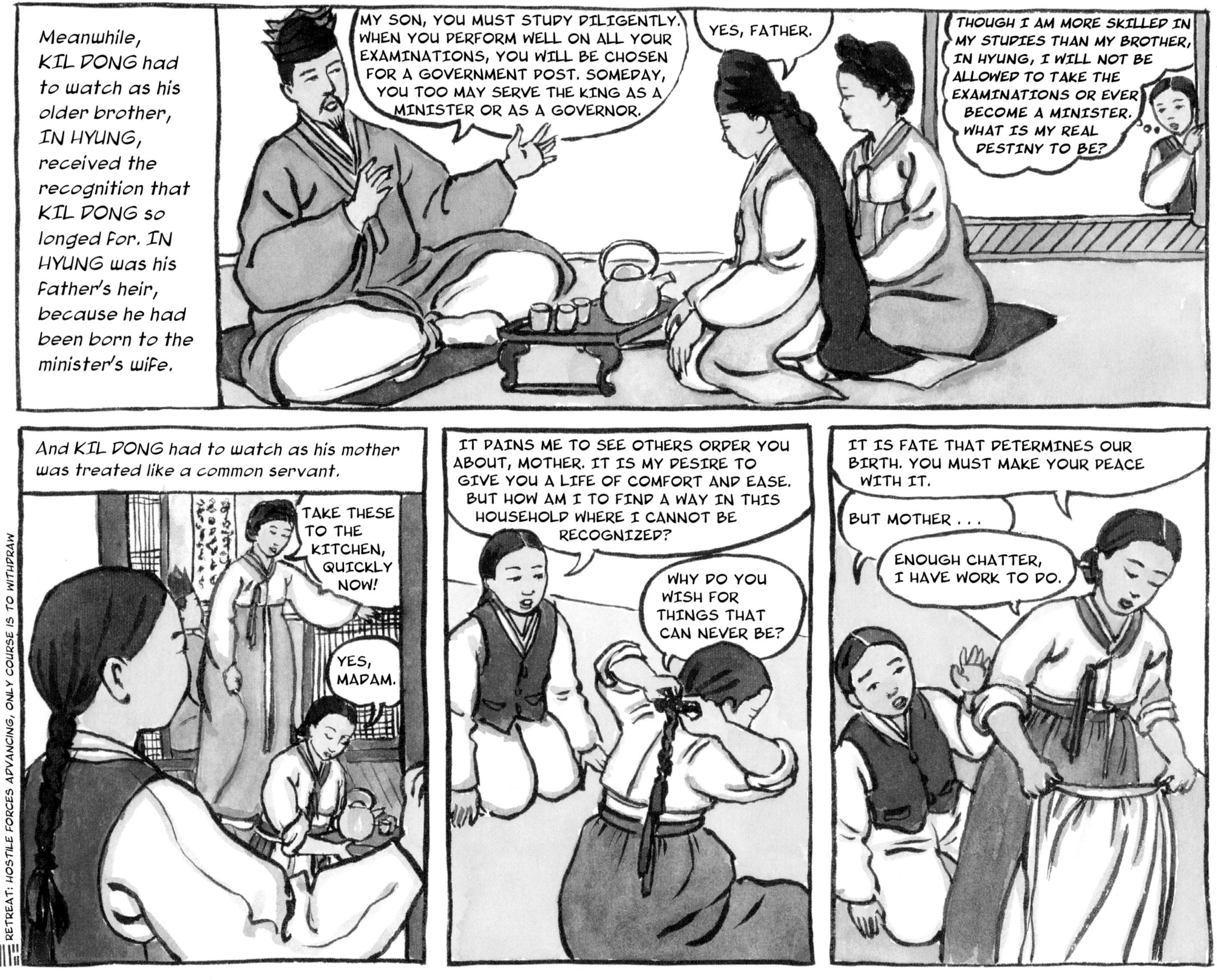
Meanwhile, KIL DONG had to watch as his older brother, IN HYUNG, received the recognition that KIL DONG so longed for. IN HYUNG was his father's heir, because he had been born to the minister's wife.
MY SON, YOU MUST STUDY DILIGENTLY. WHEN YOU PERFORM WELL ON ALL YOUR EXAMINATIONS, YOU WILL BE CHOSEN FOR A GOVERNMENT POST. SOMEDAY, YOU TOO MAY SERVE THE KING AS A MINISTER OR AS A GOVERNOR.
YES, FATHER.
THOUGH I AM MORE SKILLED IN MY STUDIES THAN MY BROTHER, IN HYUNG, I WILL NOT BE ALLOWED TO TAKE THE EXAMINATIONS OR EVER BECOME A MINISTER. WHAT IS MY REAL DESTINY TO BE?
And KIL DONG had to watch as his mother was treated like a common servant.
TAKE THESE TO THE KITCHEN, QUICKLY NOW!
YES, MADAM.
IT PAINS ME TO SEE OTHERS ORDER YOU ABOUT, MOTHER. IT IS MY DESIRE TO GIVE YOU A LIFE OF COMFORT AND EASE. BUT HOW AM I TO FIND A WAY IN THIS HOUSEHOLD WHERE I CANNOT BE RECOGNIZED?
WHY DO YOU WISH FOR THINGS THAT CAN NEVER BE?
IT IS FATE THAT DETERMINES OUR BIRTH. YOU MUST MAKE YOUR PEACE WITH IT.
BUT MOTHER . . .
ENOUGH CHATTER, I HAVE WORK TO DO.

RETREAT: HOSTILE FORCES ADVANCING, ONLY COURSE IS TO WITHDRAW

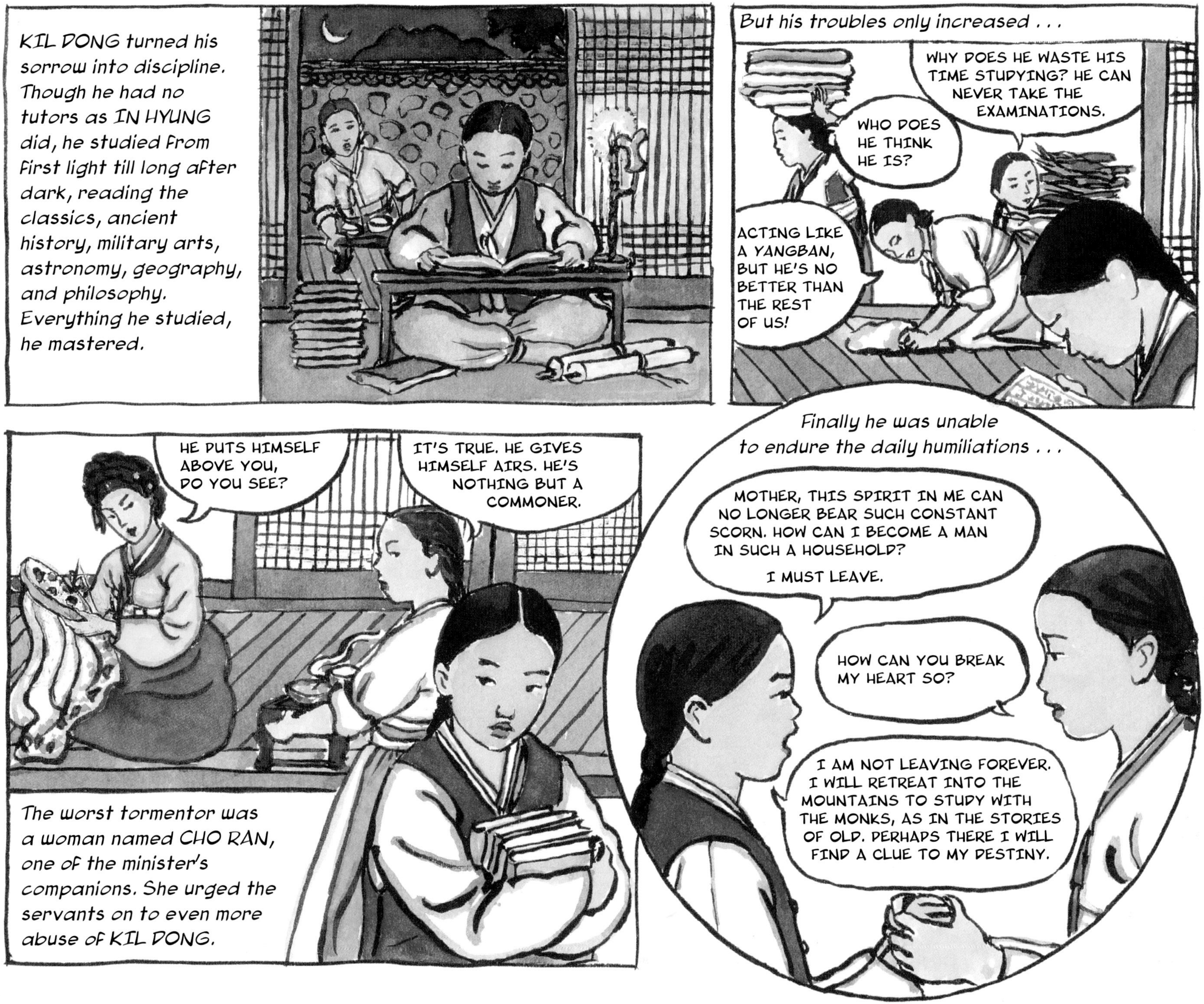
KIL DONG turned his sorrow into discipline. Though he had no tutors as IN HYUNG did, he studied from first light till long after dark, reading the classics, ancient history, military arts, astronomy, geography, and philosophy. Everything he studied, he mastered.
But his troubles only increased . . .
WHY DOES HE WASTE HIS TIME STUDYING? HE CAN NEVER TAKE THE EXAMINATIONS.
WHO DOES HE THINK HE IS?
ACTING LIKE A YANGBAN, BUT HE'S NO BETTER THAN THE REST OF US!
HE PUTS HIMSELF ABOVE YOU, DO YOU SEE?
IT'S TRUE. HE GIVES HIMSELF AIRS. HE'S NOTHING BUT A COMMONER.
The worst tormentor was a woman named CHO RAN, one of the minister's companions. She urged the servants on to even more abuse of KIL DONG.
Finally he was unable to endure the daily humiliations . . .
MOTHER, THIS SPIRIT IN ME CAN NO LONGER BEAR SUCH CONSTANT SCORN. HOW CAN I BECOME A MAN IN SUCH A HOUSEHOLD?
I MUST LEAVE.
HOW CAN YOU BREAK MY HEART SO?
I AM NOT LEAVING FOREVER. I WILL RETREAT INTO THE MOUNTAINS TO STUDY WITH THE MONKS, AS IN THE STORIES OF OLD. PERHAPS THERE I WILL FIND A CLUE TO MY DESTINY.

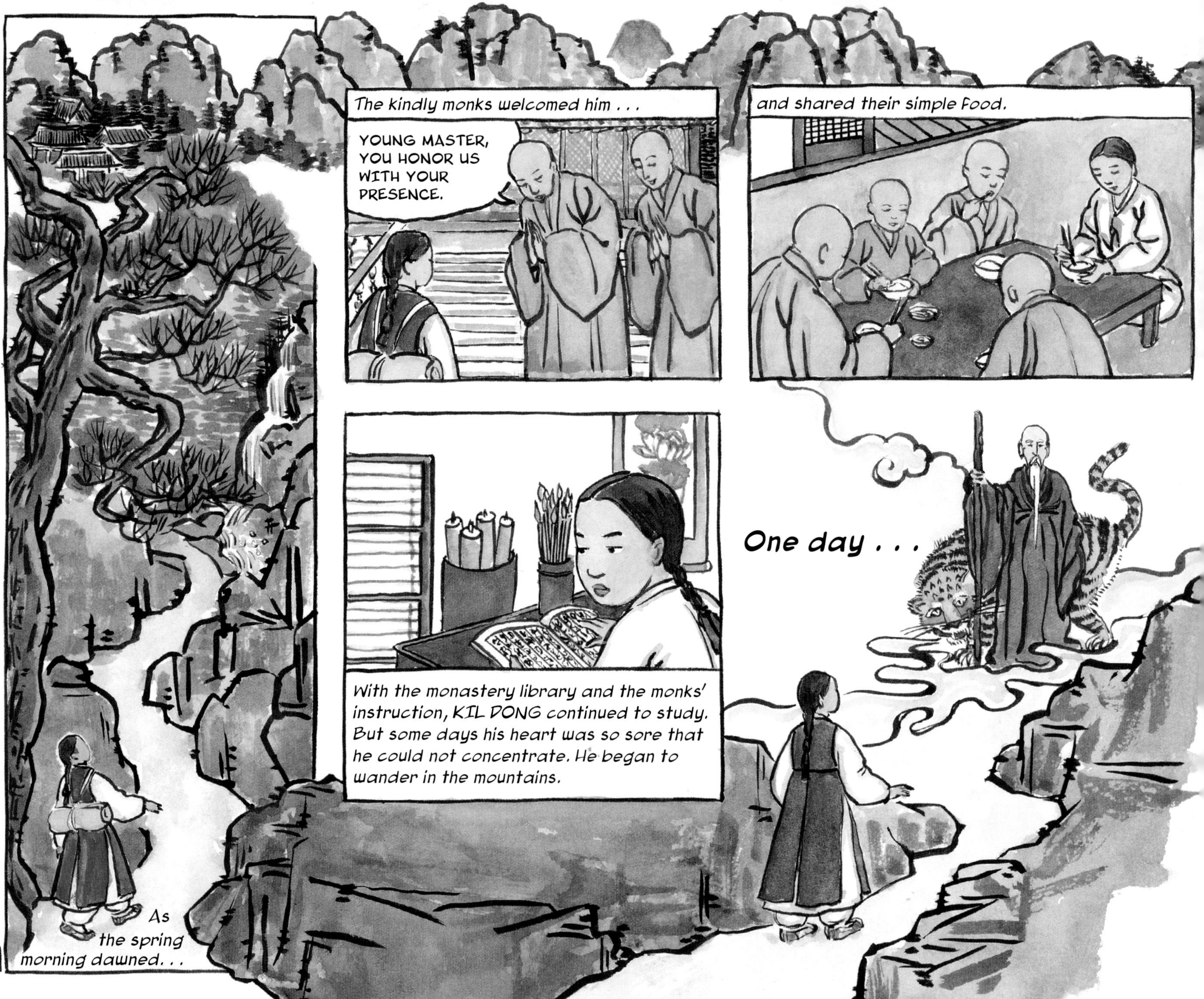
As the spring morning dawned. . .
The kindly monks welcomed him . . .
YOUNG MASTER, YOU HONOR US WITH YOUR PRESENCE.
and shared their simple food.
With the monastery library and the monks' instruction, KIL DONG continued to study. But some days his heart was so sore that he could not concentrate. He began to wander in the mountains.
One day . . .

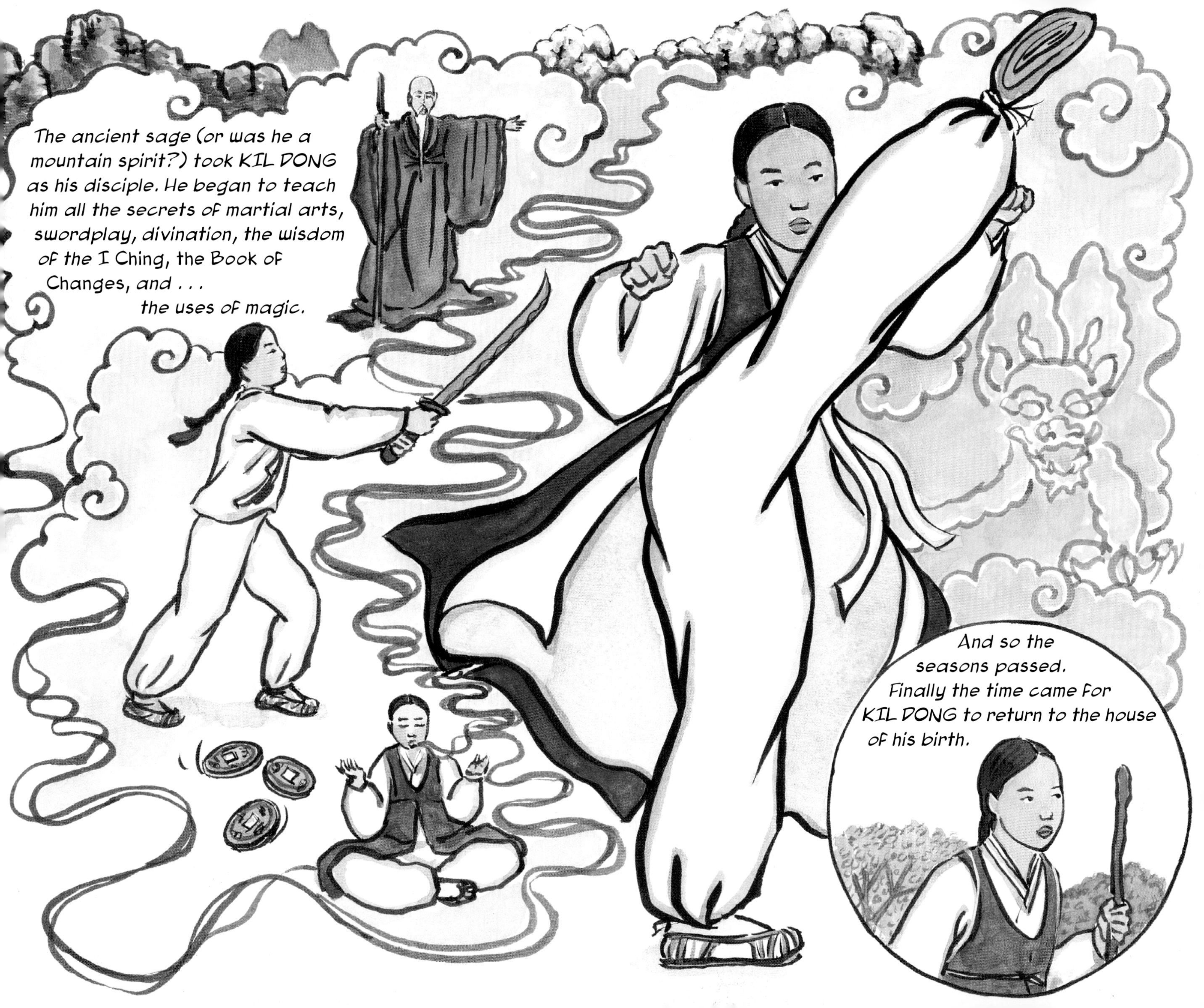
The ancient sage (or was he a mountain spirit?) took KIL DONG as his disciple. He began to teach him all the secrets of martial arts, swordplay, divination, the wisdom of the I Ching, the Book of Changes, and . . . the uses of magic.
And so the seasons passed. Finally the time came for KIL DONG to return to the house of his birth.

But at the minister's house, KIL DONG was still the object of scorn. Night after night, his tormented spirit drove him outside to practice his skills and release his frustration, the frustration that no magic could cure. One night, under a bright spring moon . . .
HE HAS GROWN IN SKILL AND STRENGTH FAR BEYOND IN HYUNG, WHOSE PLACE IN THE WORLD IS SECURE. WHAT IS TO BECOME OF KIL DONG?

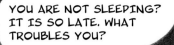

YOU ARE NOT SLEEPING? IT IS SO LATE. WHAT TROUBLES YOU?

I CANNOT SLEEP FOR SORROW. I CAN NEVER BE CALLED A MAN.

WHAT DO YOU MEAN?

THOUGH I AM GRATEFUL FOR ALL YOU HAVE GIVEN ME, MY LIFE HAS ONE GREAT SADNESS. HOW CAN I BECOME A MAN WHEN I CANNOT EVEN CLAIM MY OWN FATHER?

HOW DARE YOU SPEAK THIS WAY? YOU'RE NOT THE FIRST CHILD BORN TO A MAID IN A NOBLEMAN'S HOUSE! IF YOU SPEAK SO ARROGANTLY AGAIN, I WILL FORBID YOU TO BE IN MY PRESENCE.

MY REJECTION TORMENTS HIM, BUT WHAT CAN BE DONE? THE LAW IS CLEAR: THE BOY CAN NEVER BE RECOGNIZED AS A YANGBAN. WHAT CRUEL TWIST OF FATE IS THIS, THAT SUCH TALENT CAN NEVER BE USED IN SERVICE TO THE KING?

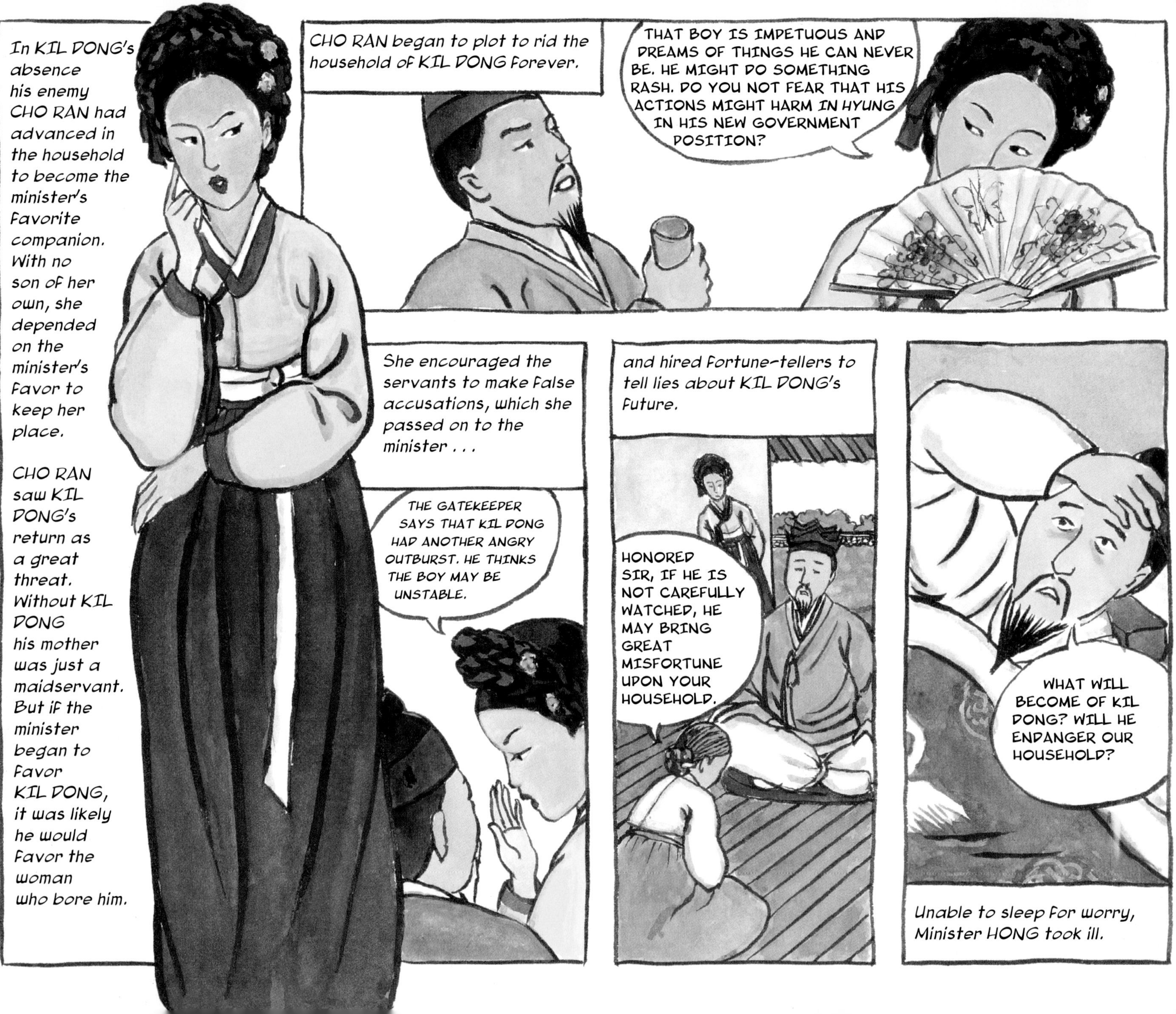
In KIL DONG's absence his enemy CHO RAN had advanced in the household to become the minister's favorite companion. With no son of her own, she depended on the minister's favor to keep her place.
CHO RAN saw KIL DONG's return as a great threat. Without KIL DONG his mother was just a maidservant. But if the minister began to favor KIL DONG, it was likely he would favor the woman who bore him.
CHO RAN began to plot to rid the household of KIL DONG forever.
THAT BOY IS IMPETUOUS AND DREAMS OF THINGS HE CAN NEVER BE. HE MIGHT DO SOMETHING RASH. DO YOU NOT FEAR THAT HIS ACTIONS MIGHT HARM IN HYUNG IN HIS NEW GOVERNMENT POSITION?
She encouraged the servants to make false accusations, which she passed on to the minister . . .
THE GATEKEEPER SAYS THAT KIL DONG HAD ANOTHER ANGRY OUTBURST. HE THINKS THE BOY MAY BE UNSTABLE.
and hired fortune-tellers to tell lies about KIL DONG's future.
HONORED SIR, IF HE IS NOT CAREFULLY WATCHED, HE MAY BRING GREAT MISFORTUNE UPON YOUR HOUSEHOLD.
WHAT WILL BECOME OF KIL DONG? WILL HE ENDANGER OUR HOUSEHOLD?
Unable to sleep for worry, Minister HONG took ill.

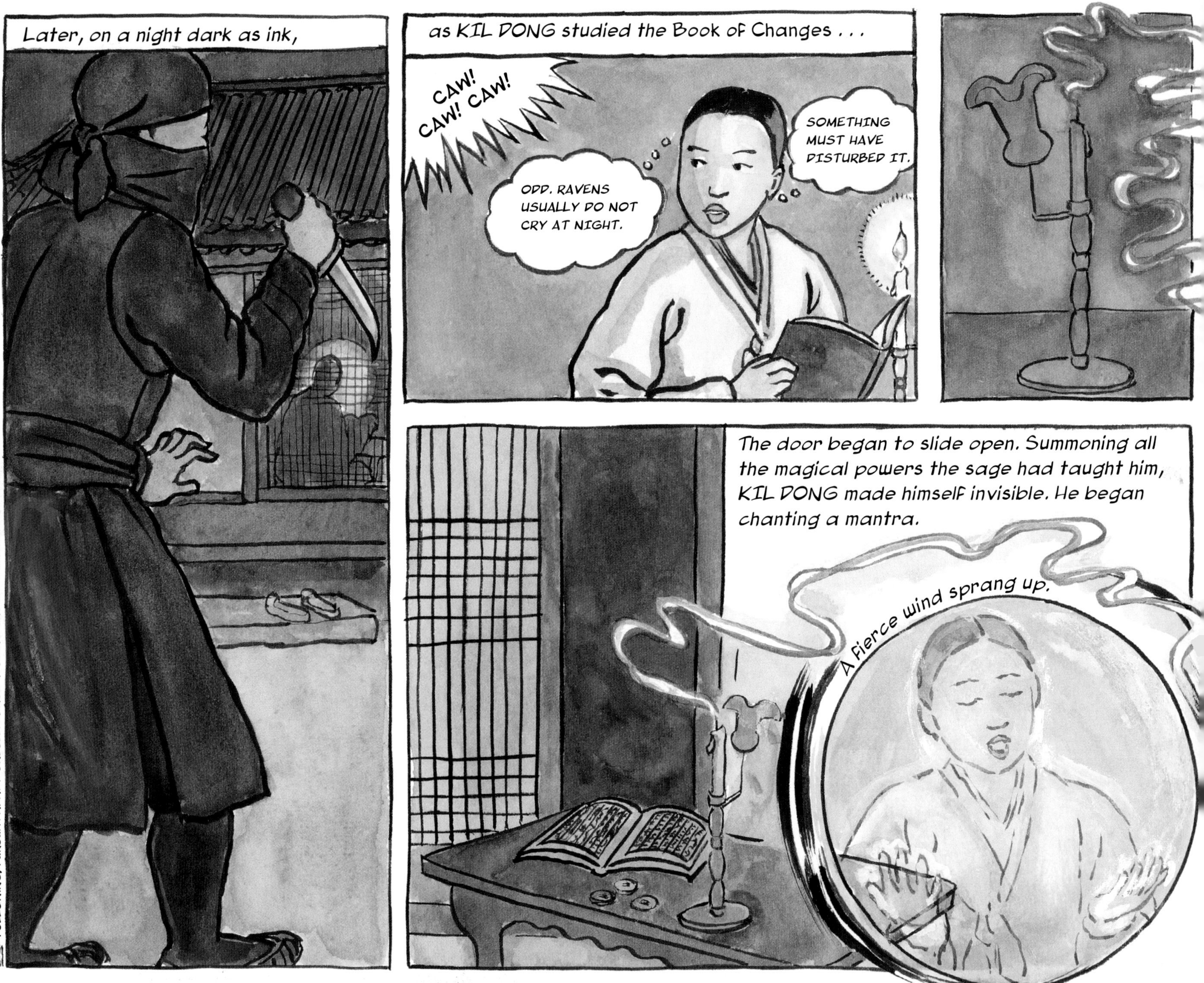
Later, on a night dark as ink,
as KIL DONG studied the Book of Changes . . .
CAW! CAW! CAW!
ODD. RAVENS USUALLY DO NOT CRY AT NIGHT.
SOMETHING MUST HAVE DISTURBED IT.
The door began to slide open. Summoning all the magical powers the sage had taught him, KIL DONG made himself invisible. He began chanting a mantra.
A fierce wind sprang up.

FOLLOWING/PURSUIT: ADAPT ONESELF. BASE 9: BEING CROSSED ON LEAVING HOME

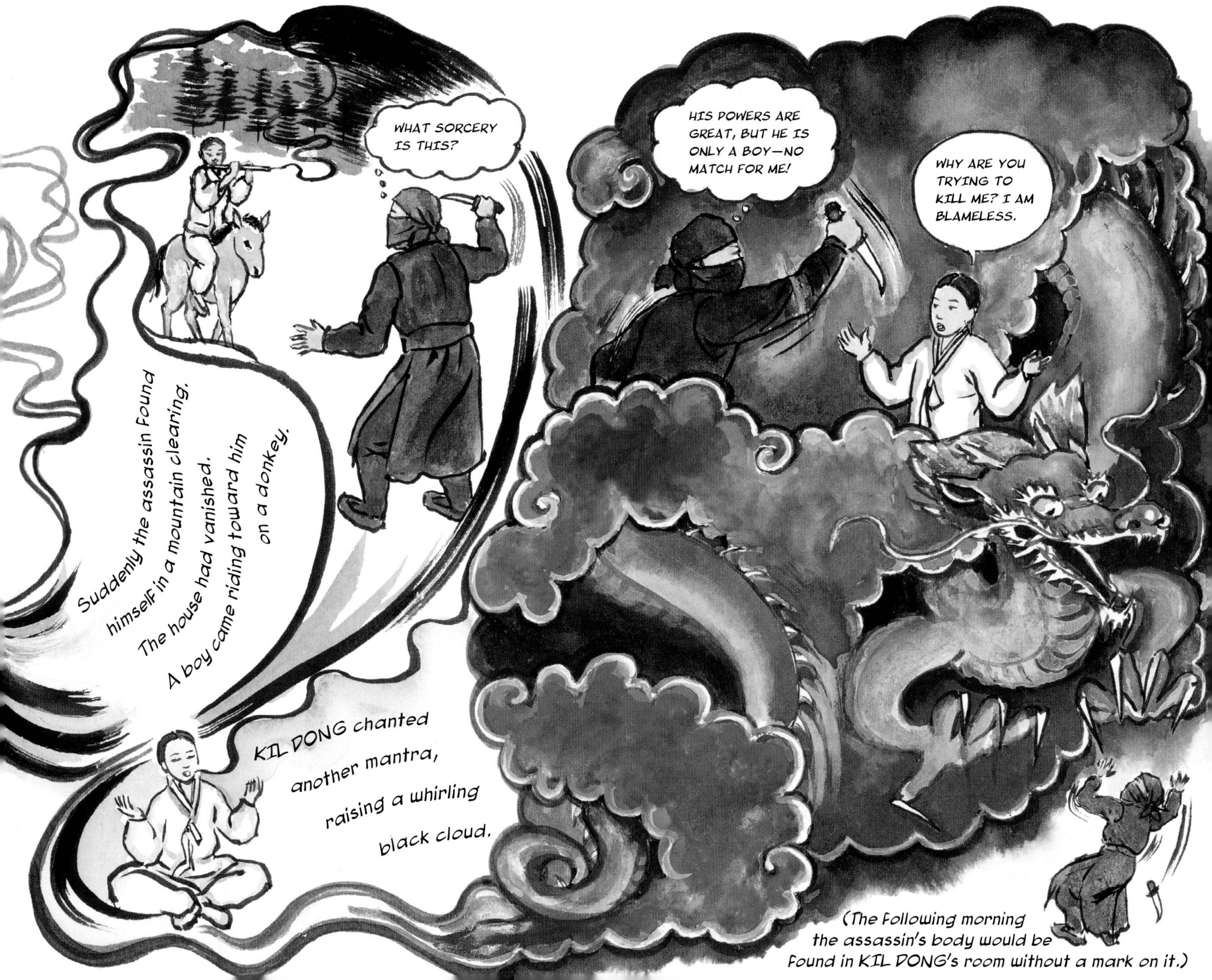
Suddenly the assassin found himself in a mountain clearing. The house had vanished. A boy came riding toward him on a donkey.
WHAT SORCERY IS THIS?
KIL DONG chanted another mantra, raising a whirling black cloud.
HIS POWERS ARE GREAT, BUT HE IS ONLY A BOY—NO MATCH FOR ME!
WHY ARE YOU TRYING TO KILL ME? I AM BLAMELESS.
(The following morning the assassin's body would be found in KIL DONG's room without a mark on it.)

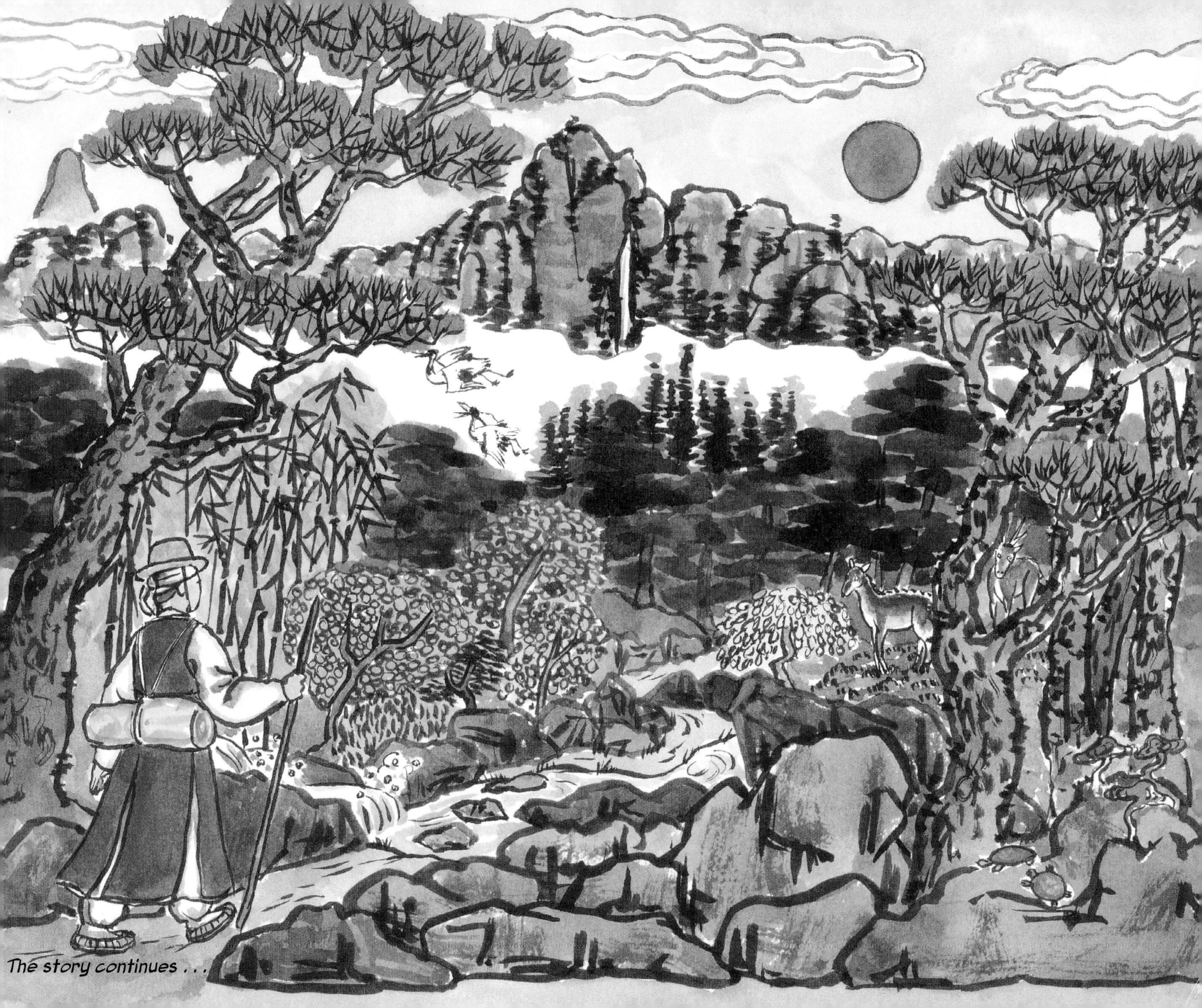
The story continues . . .

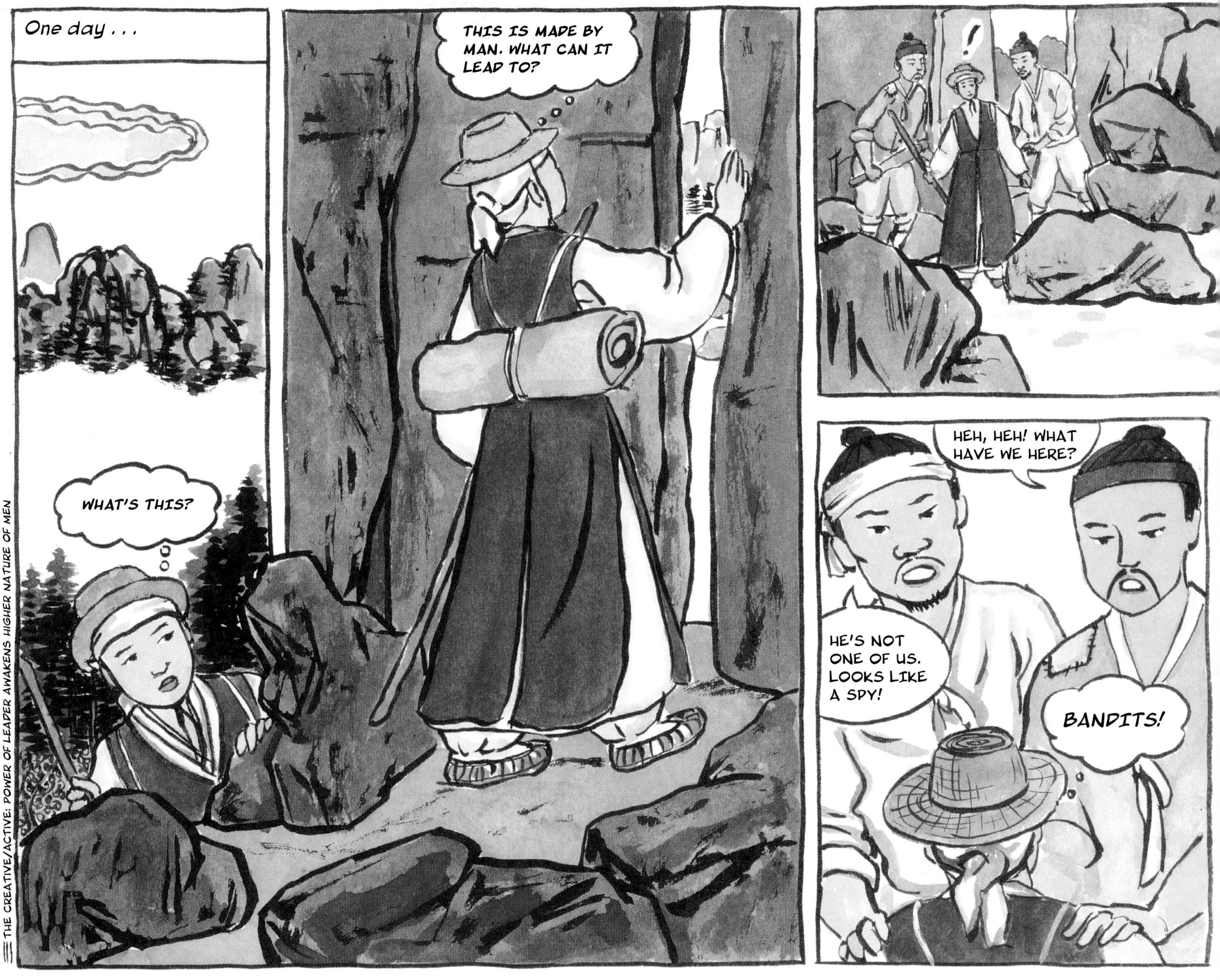
One day . . .
WHAT'S THIS?
THIS IS MADE BY MAN. WHAT CAN IT LEAD TO?
!
HEH, HEH! WHAT HAVE WE HERE?
HE'S NOT ONE OF US. LOOKS LIKE A SPY!
BANDITS!

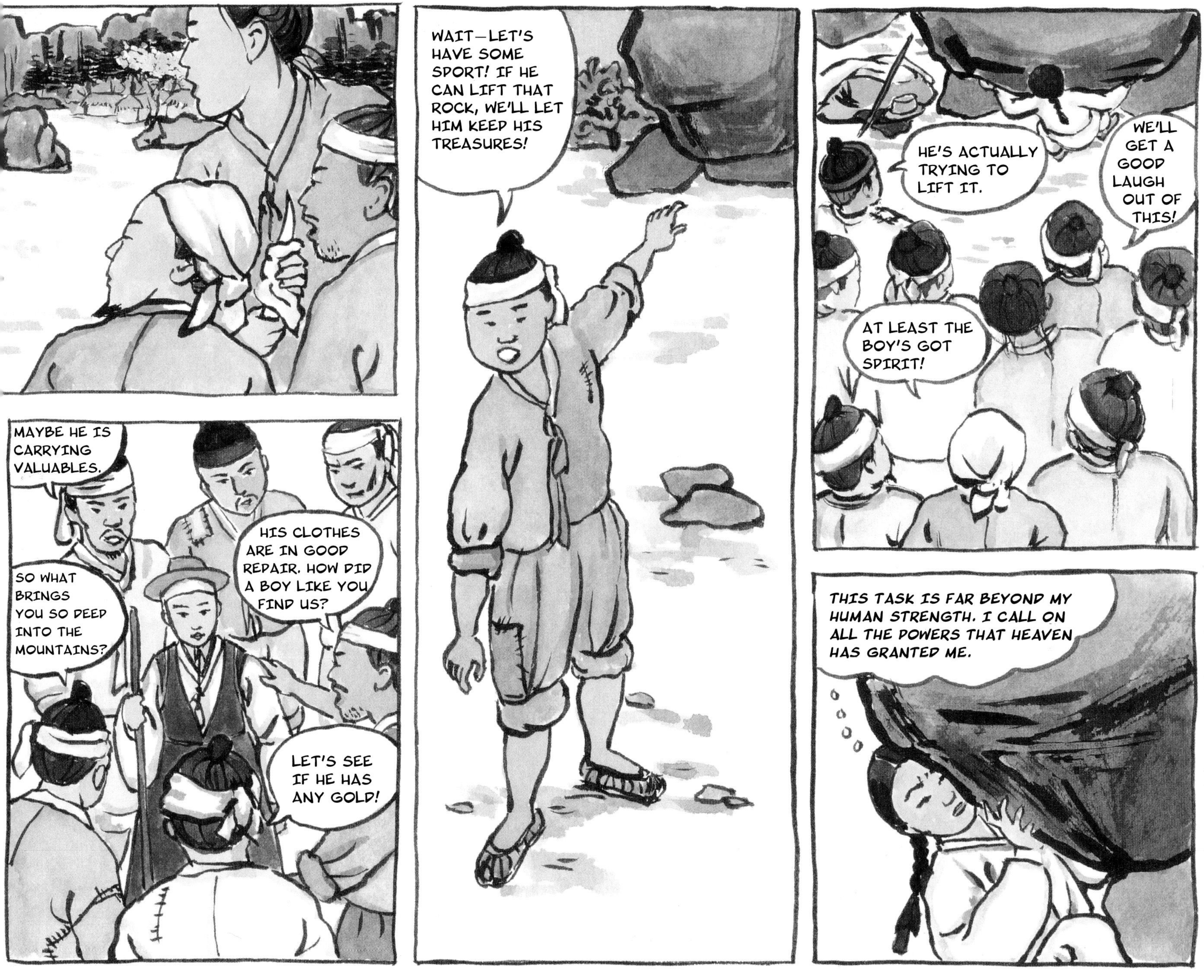
MAYBE HE IS CARRYING VALUABLES.
SO WHAT BRINGS YOU SO DEEP INTO THE MOUNTAINS?
HIS CLOTHES ARE IN GOOD REPAIR. HOW DID A BOY LIKE YOU FIND US?
LET'S SEE IF HE HAS ANY GOLD!
WAIT—LET'S HAVE SOME SPORT! IF HE CAN LIFT THAT ROCK, WE'LL LET HIM KEEP HIS TREASURES!
HE'S ACTUALLY TRYING TO LIFT IT.
WE'LL GET A GOOD LAUGH OUT OF THIS!
AT LEAST THE BOY'S GOT SPIRIT!
THIS TASK IS FAR BEYOND MY HUMAN STRENGTH. I CALL ON ALL THE POWERS THAT HEAVEN HAS GRANTED ME.

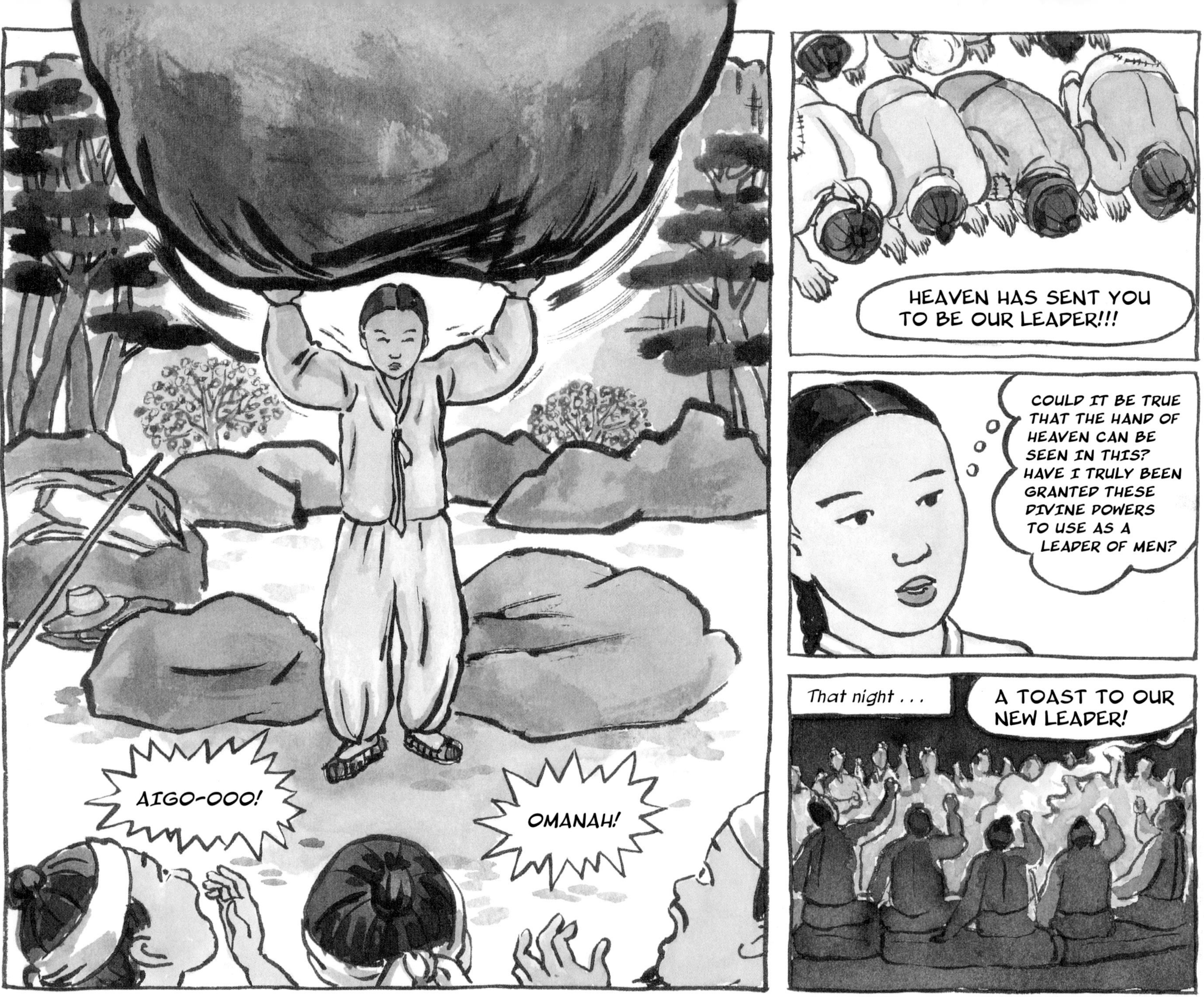
AIGO-OOO!
OMANAH!
HEAVEN HAS SENT YOU TO BE OUR LEADER!!!
COULD IT BE TRUE THAT THE HAND OF HEAVEN CAN BE SEEN IN THIS? HAVE I TRULY BEEN GRANTED THESE DIVINE POWERS TO USE AS A LEADER OF MEN?
That night . . .
A TOAST TO OUR NEW LEADER!

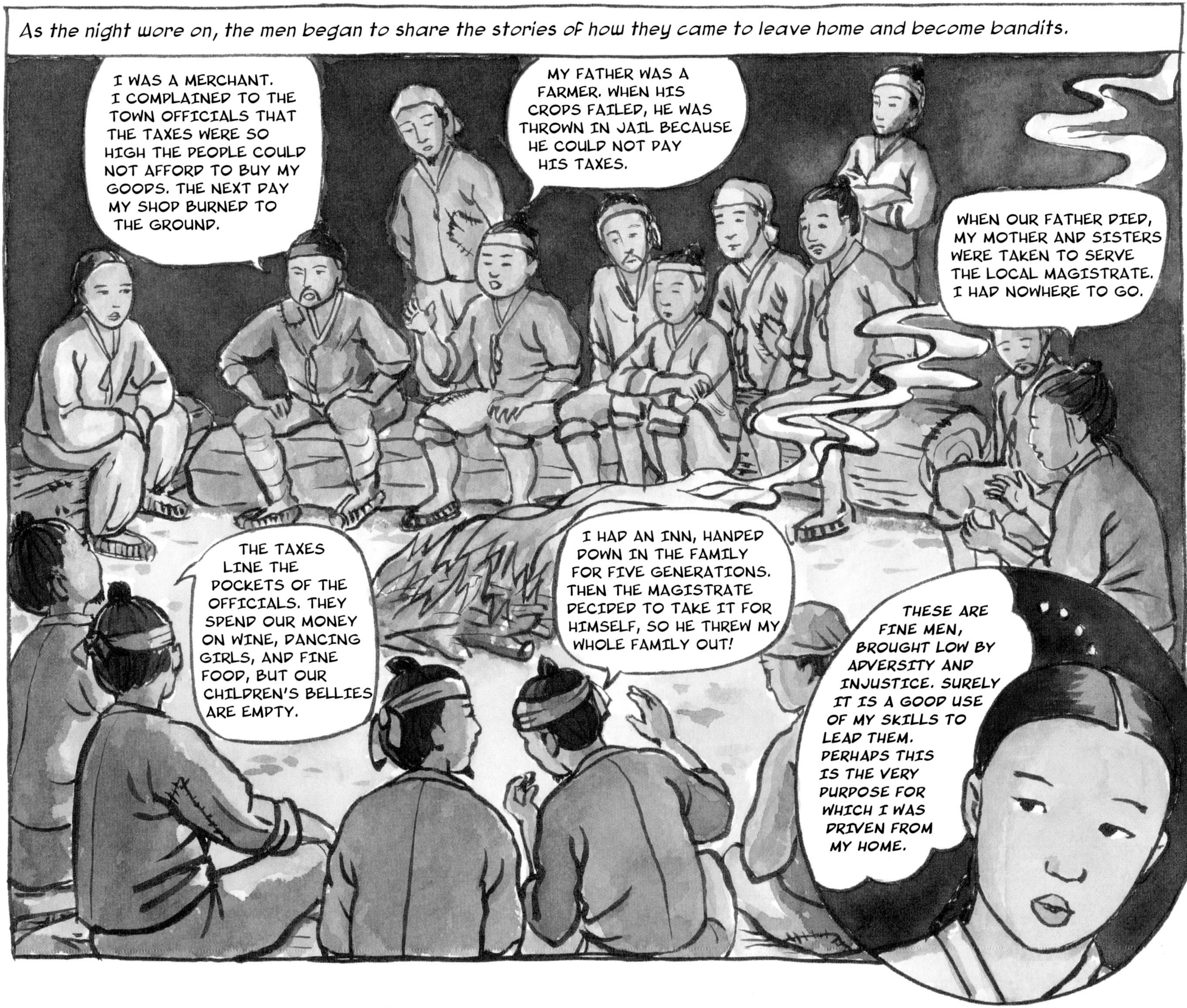
As the night wore on, the men began to share the stories of how they came to leave home and become bandits.
I WAS A MERCHANT. I COMPLAINED TO THE TOWN OFFICIALS THAT THE TAXES WERE SO HIGH THE PEOPLE COULD NOT AFFORD TO BUY MY GOODS. THE NEXT DAY MY SHOP BURNED TO THE GROUND.
MY FATHER WAS A FARMER. WHEN HIS CROPS FAILED, HE WAS THROWN IN JAIL BECAUSE HE COULD NOT PAY HIS TAXES.
WHEN OUR FATHER DIED, MY MOTHER AND SISTERS WERE TAKEN TO SERVE THE LOCAL MAGISTRATE. I HAD NOWHERE TO GO.
THE TAXES LINE THE POCKETS OF THE OFFICIALS. THEY SPEND OUR MONEY ON WINE, DANCING GIRLS, AND FINE FOOD, BUT OUR CHILDREN'S BELLIES ARE EMPTY.
I HAD AN INN, HANDED DOWN IN THE FAMILY FOR FIVE GENERATIONS. THEN THE MAGISTRATE DECIDED TO TAKE IT FOR HIMSELF, SO HE THREW MY WHOLE FAMILY OUT!
THESE ARE FINE MEN, BROUGHT LOW BY ADVERSITY AND INJUSTICE. SURELY IT IS A GOOD USE OF MY SKILLS TO LEAD THEM. PERHAPS THIS IS THE VERY PURPOSE FOR WHICH I WAS DRIVEN FROM MY HOME.

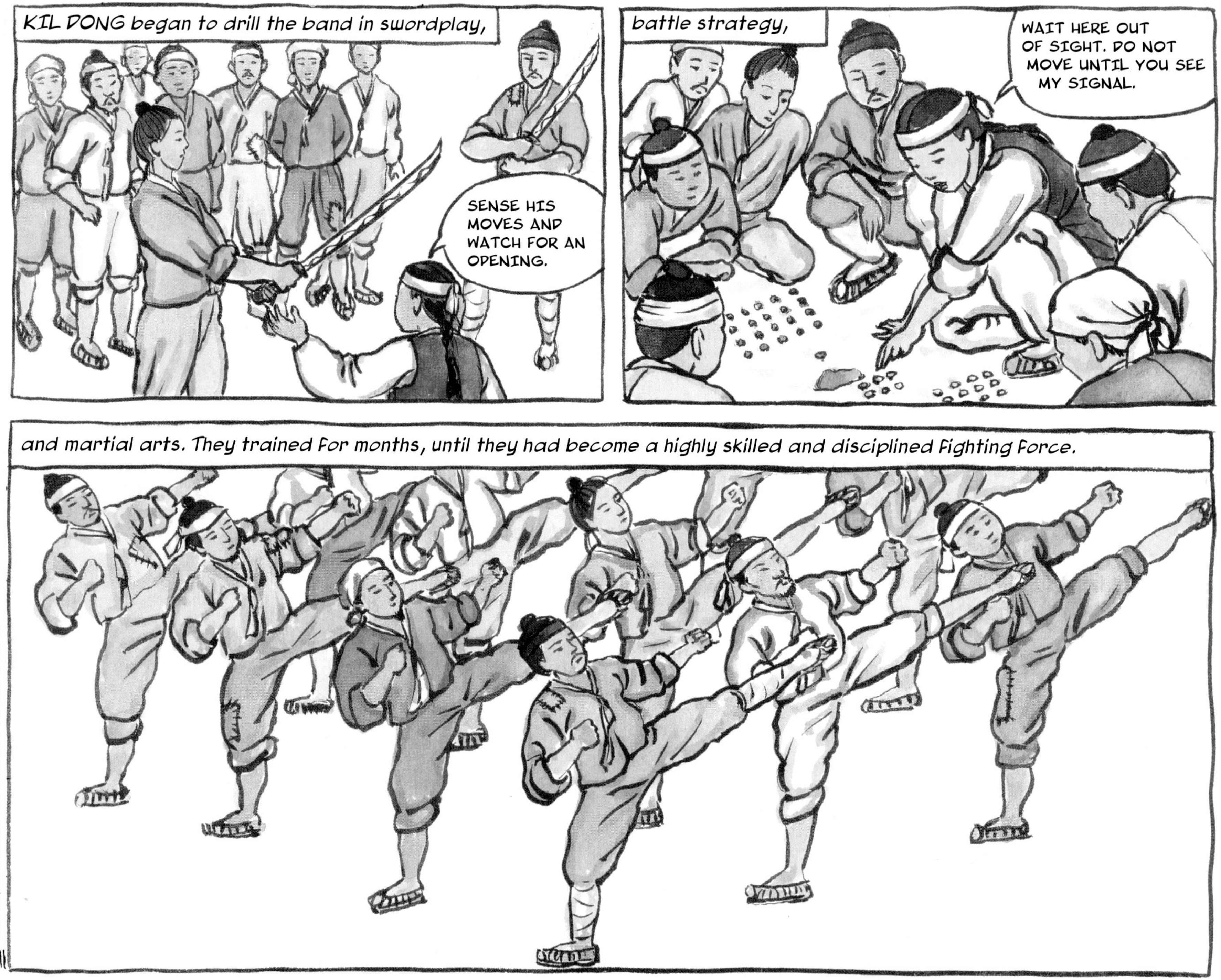
KIL DONG began to drill the band in swordplay,
SENSE HIS MOVES AND WATCH FOR AN OPENING.
battle strategy,
WAIT HERE OUT OF SIGHT. DO NOT MOVE UNTIL YOU SEE MY SIGNAL.
and martial arts. They trained for months, until they had become a highly skilled and disciplined fighting force.

WAITING/ATTENDING: FORTIFICATION TO FACE DANGER

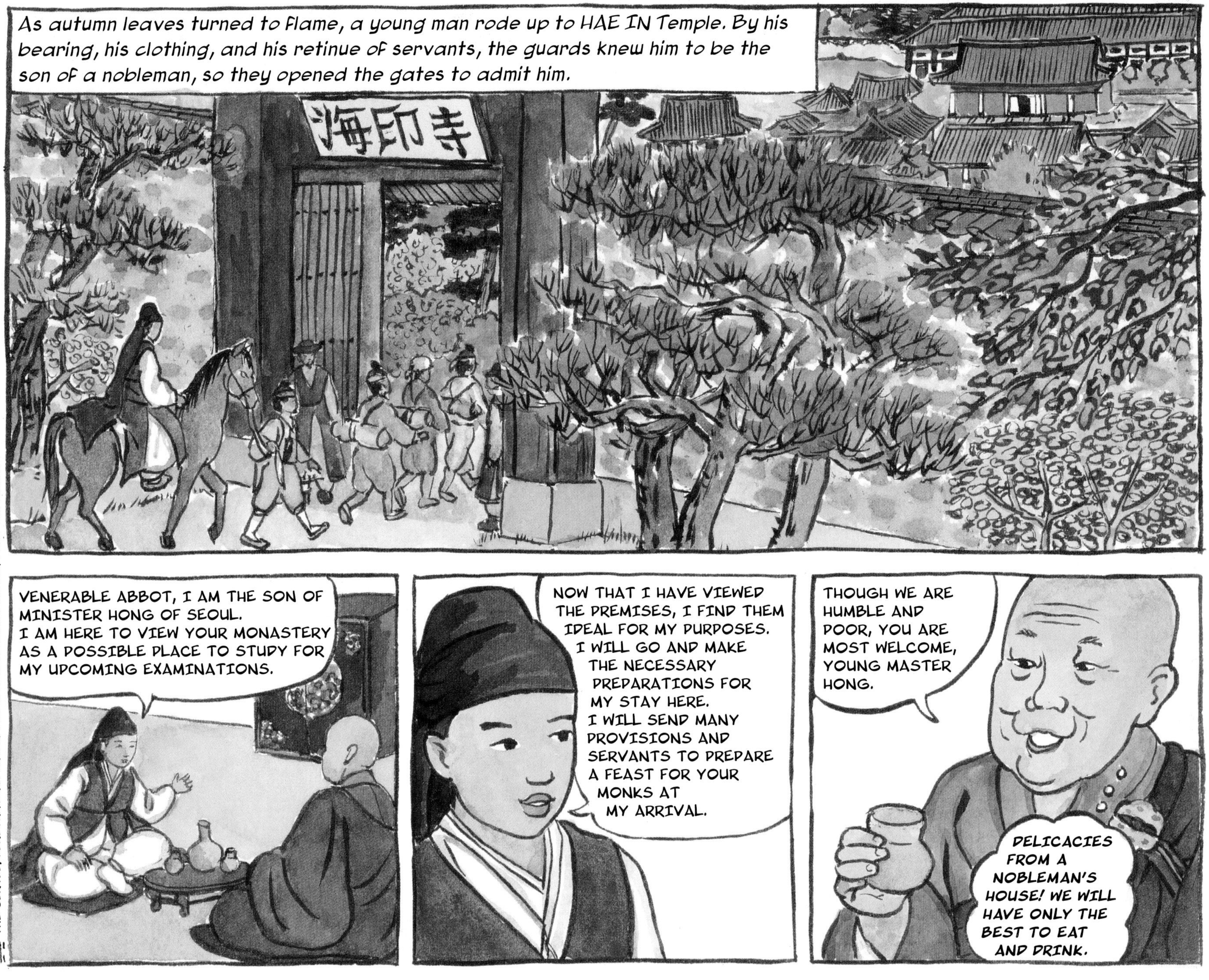
As autumn leaves turned to flame, a young man rode up to HAE IN Temple. By his bearing, his clothing, and his retinue of servants, the guards knew him to be the son of a nobleman, so they opened the gates to admit him.
海印寺
VENERABLE ABBOT, I AM THE SON OF MINISTER HONG OF SEOUL. I AM HERE TO VIEW YOUR MONASTERY AS A POSSIBLE PLACE TO STUDY FOR MY UPCOMING EXAMINATIONS.
NOW THAT I HAVE VIEWED THE PREMISES, I FIND THEM IDEAL FOR MY PURPOSES. I WILL GO AND MAKE THE NECESSARY PREPARATIONS FOR MY STAY HERE. I WILL SEND MANY PROVISIONS AND SERVANTS TO PREPARE A FEAST FOR YOUR MONKS AT MY ARRIVAL.
THOUGH WE ARE HUMBLE AND POOR, YOU ARE MOST WELCOME, YOUNG MASTER HONG.
DELICACIES FROM A NOBLEMAN'S HOUSE! WE WILL HAVE ONLY THE BEST TO EAT AND DRINK.

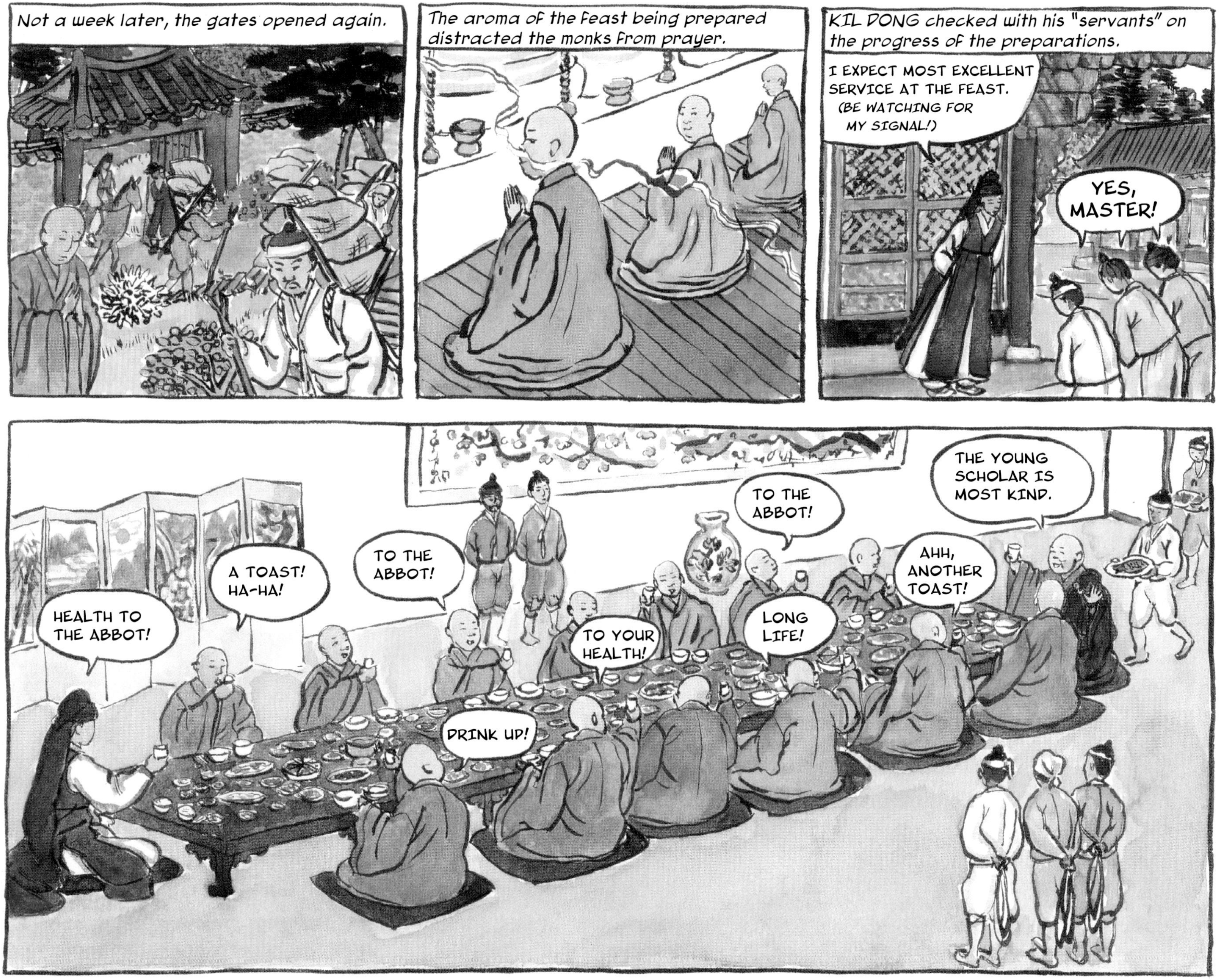
Not a week later, the gates opened again.
The aroma of the feast being prepared distracted the monks from prayer.
KIL DONG checked with his "servants" on the progress of the preparations.
I EXPECT MOST EXCELLENT SERVICE AT THE FEAST. (BE WATCHING FOR MY SIGNAL!)
YES, MASTER!
HEALTH TO THE ABBOT!
A TOAST! HA-HA!
TO THE ABBOT!
TO YOUR HEALTH!
TO THE ABBOT!
LONG LIFE!
AHH, ANOTHER TOAST!
THE YOUNG SCHOLAR IS MOST KIND.
DRINK UP!

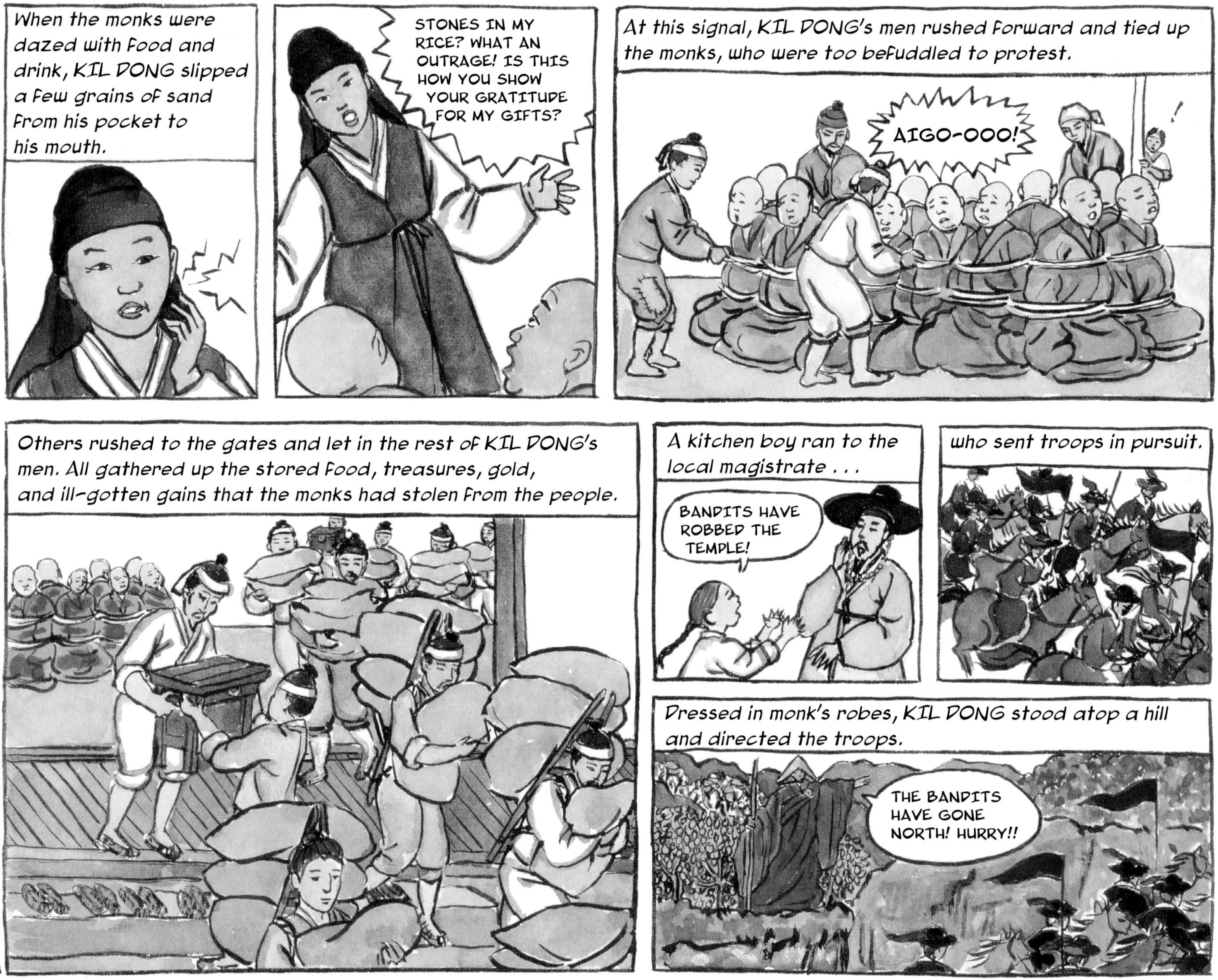
When the monks were dazed with food and drink, KIL DONG slipped a few grains of sand from his pocket to his mouth.
STONES IN MY RICE? WHAT AN OUTRAGE! IS THIS HOW YOU SHOW YOUR GRATITUDE FOR MY GIFTS?
At this signal, KIL DONG's men rushed forward and tied up the monks, who were too befuddled to protest.
AIGO-OOO!
Others rushed to the gates and let in the rest of KIL DONG's men. All gathered up the stored food, treasures, gold, and ill-gotten gains that the monks had stolen from the people.
A kitchen boy ran to the local magistrate . . .
BANDITS HAVE ROBBED THE TEMPLE!
who sent troops in pursuit.
Dressed in monk's robes, KIL DONG stood atop a hill and directed the troops.
THE BANDITS HAVE GONE NORTH! HURRY!!

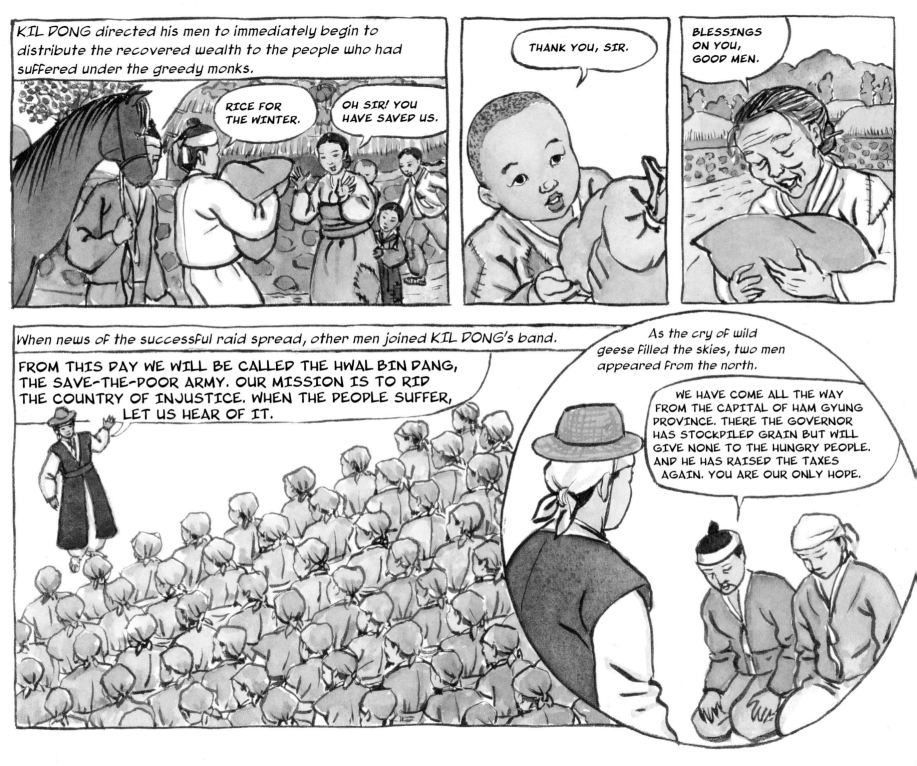

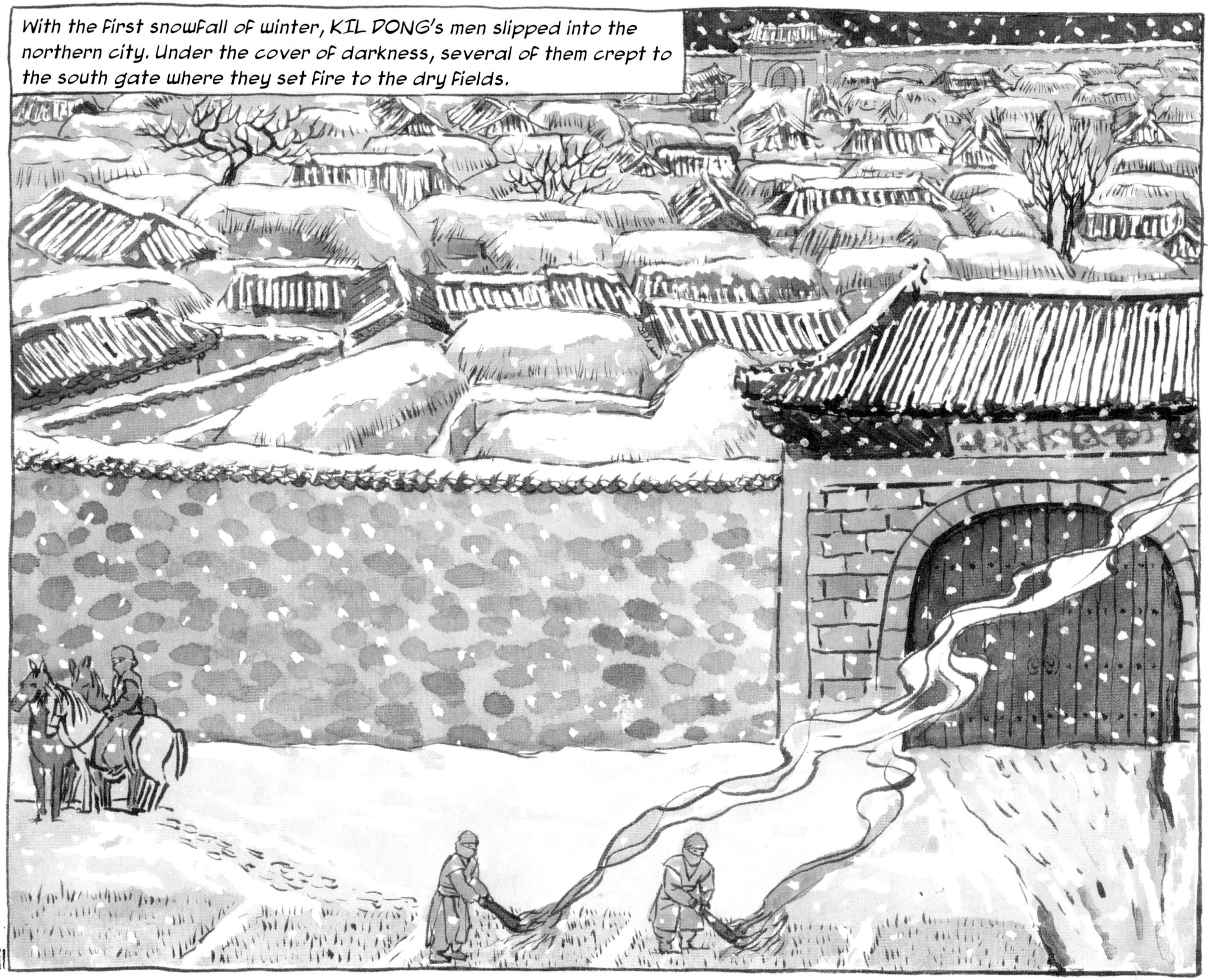
With the first snowfall of winter, KIL DONG's men slipped into the northern city. Under the cover of darkness, several of them crept to the south gate where they set fire to the dry fields.

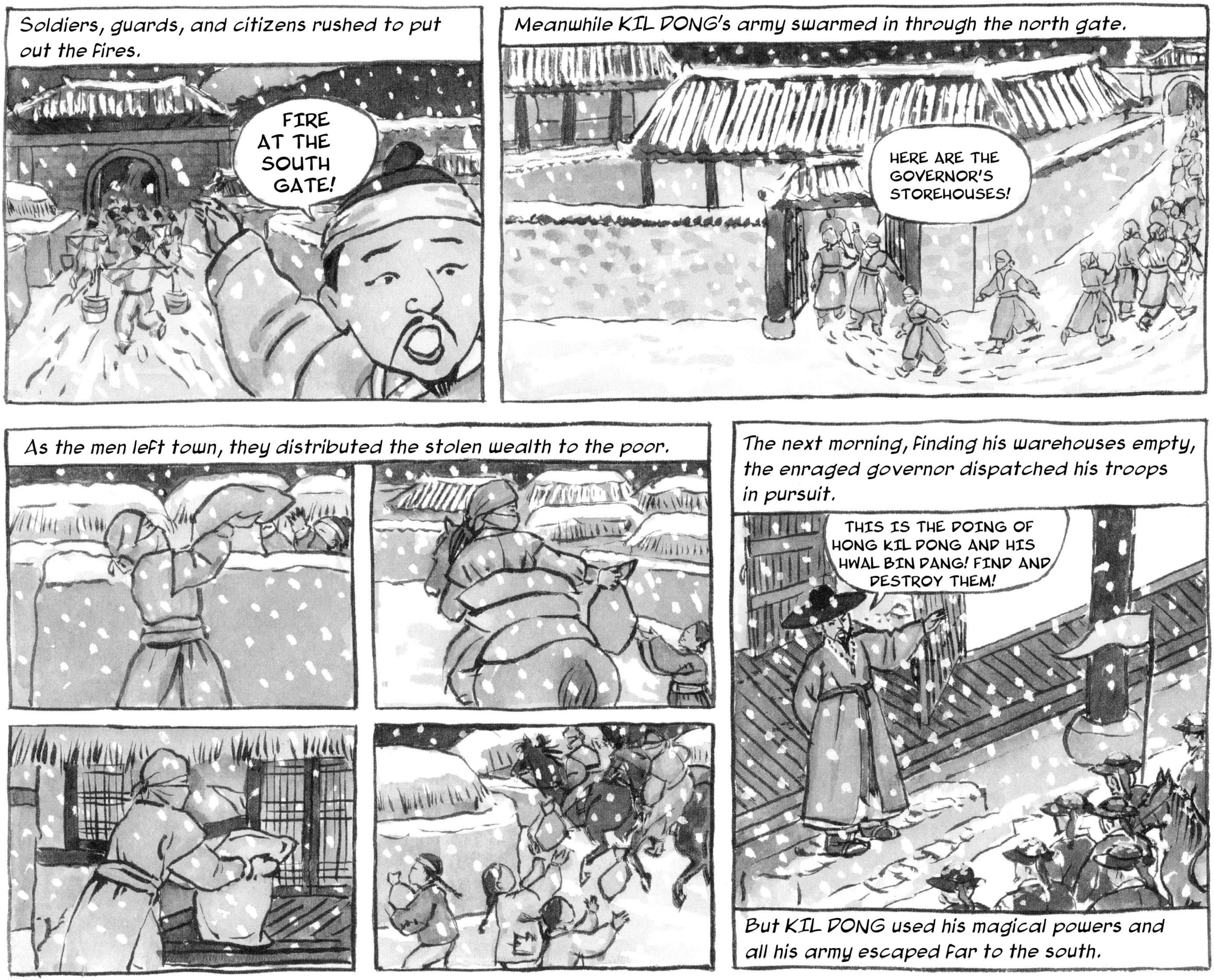
Soldiers, guards, and citizens rushed to put out the fires.
FIRE AT THE SOUTH GATE!
Meanwhile KIL DONG's army swarmed in through the north gate.
HERE ARE THE GOVERNOR'S STOREHOUSES!
As the men left town, they distributed the stolen wealth to the poor.
The next morning, finding his warehouses empty, the enraged governor dispatched his troops in pursuit.
THIS IS THE DOING OF HONG KIL DONG AND HIS HWAL BIN DANG! FIND AND DESTROY THEM!
But KIL DONG used his magical powers and all his army escaped far to the south.

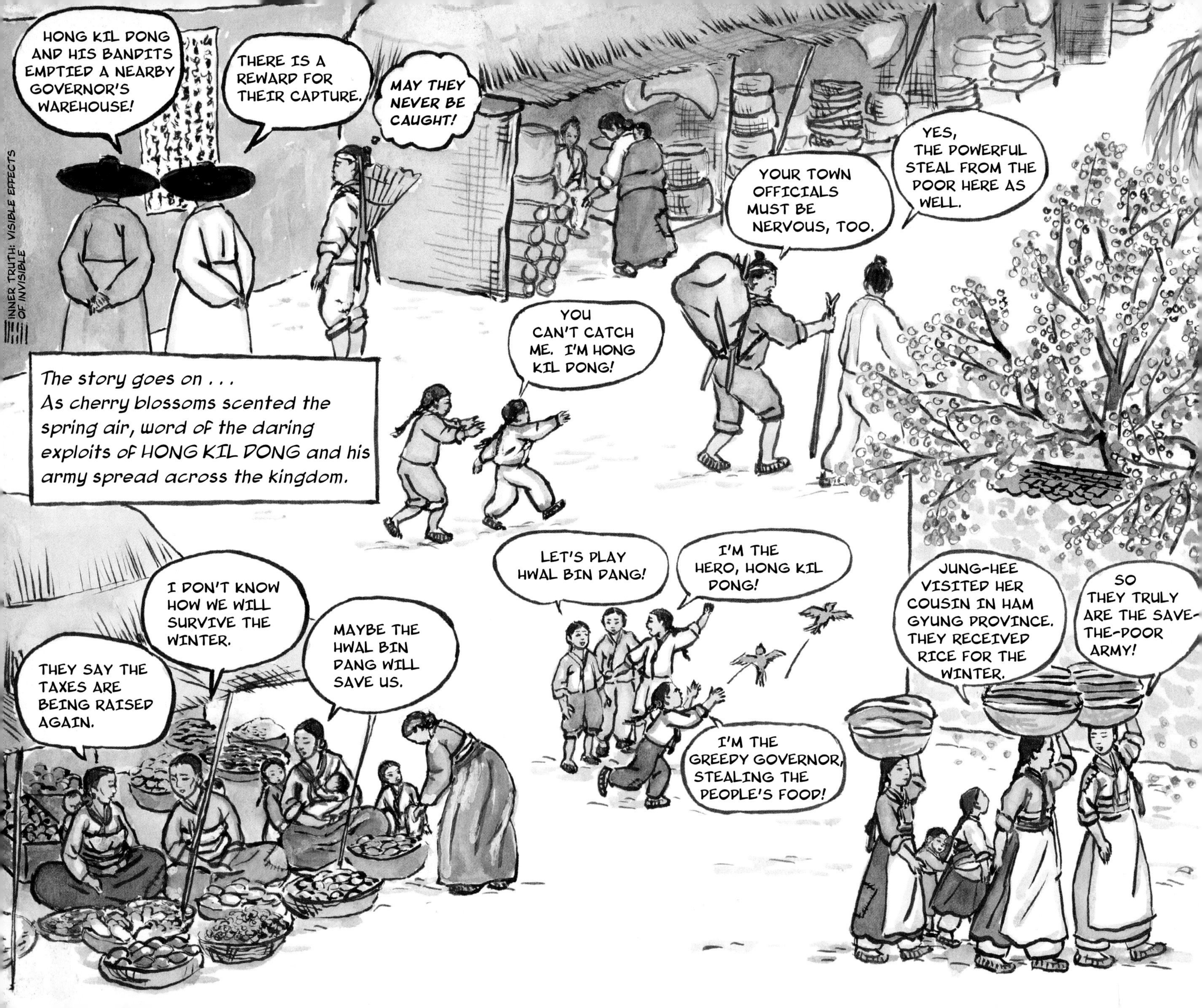
HONG KIL DONG AND HIS BANDITS EMPTIED A NEARBY GOVERNOR'S WAREHOUSE!
THERE IS A REWARD FOR THEIR CAPTURE.
MAY THEY NEVER BE CAUGHT!
YOUR TOWN OFFICIALS MUST BE NERVOUS, TOO.
YES, THE POWERFUL STEAL FROM THE POOR HERE AS WELL.
INNER TRUTH: VISIBLE EFFECTS OF INVISIBLE
The story goes on . . .
As cherry blossoms scented the spring air, word of the daring exploits of HONG KIL DONG and his army spread across the kingdom.
YOU CAN'T CATCH ME. I'M HONG KIL DONG!
LET'S PLAY HWAL BIN DANG!
I'M THE HERO, HONG KIL DONG!
I'M THE GREEDY GOVERNOR, STEALING THE PEOPLE'S FOOD!
I DON'T KNOW HOW WE WILL SURVIVE THE WINTER.
THEY SAY THE TAXES ARE BEING RAISED AGAIN.
MAYBE THE HWAL BIN DANG WILL SAVE US.
JUNG-HEE VISITED HER COUSIN IN HAM GYUNG PROVINCE. THEY RECEIVED RICE FOR THE WINTER.
SO THEY TRULY ARE THE SAVE-THE-POOR ARMY!

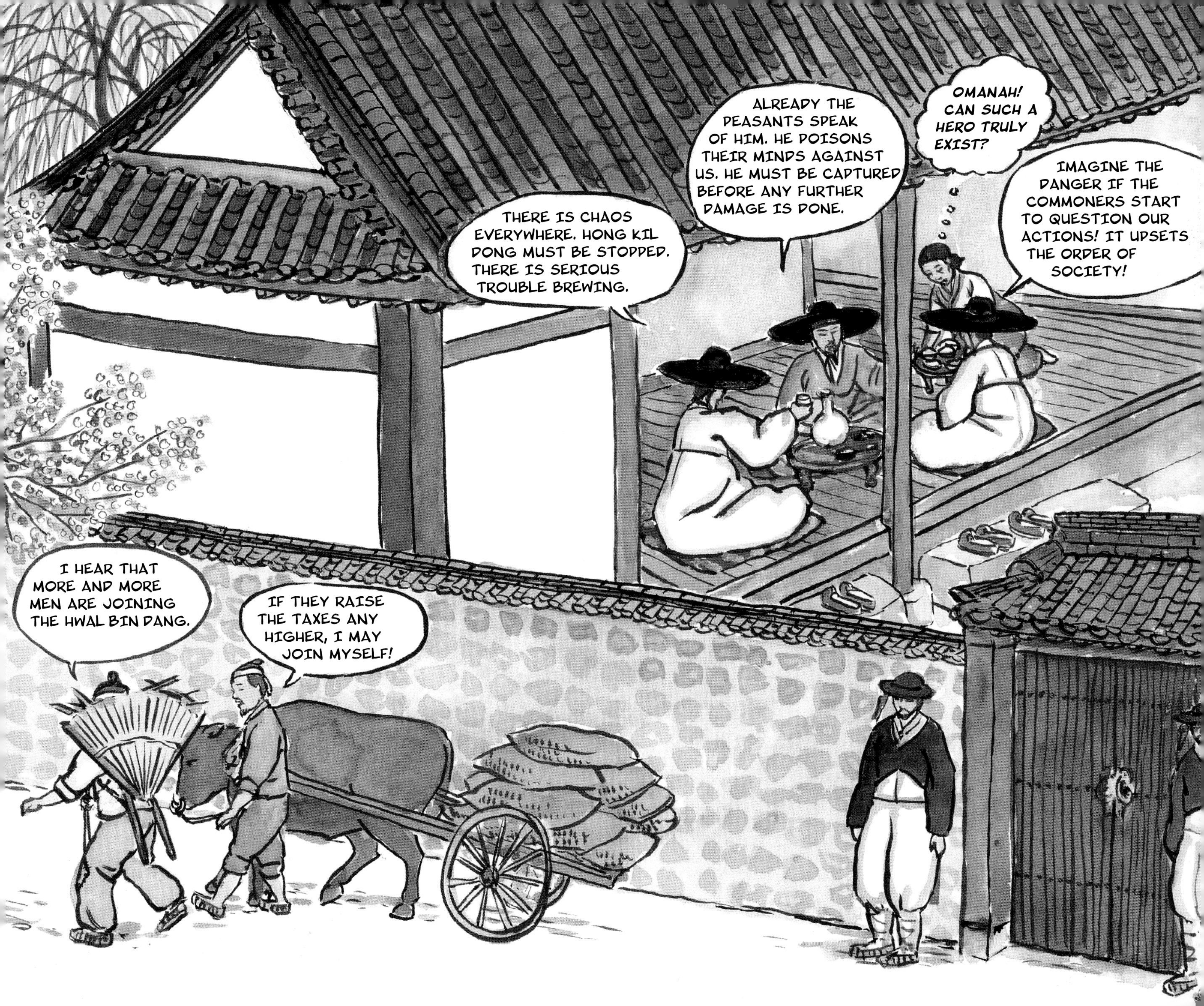
THERE IS CHAOS EVERYWHERE. HONG KIL DONG MUST BE STOPPED. THERE IS SERIOUS TROUBLE BREWING.
ALREADY THE PEASANTS SPEAK OF HIM. HE POISONS THEIR MINDS AGAINST US. HE MUST BE CAPTURED BEFORE ANY FURTHER DAMAGE IS DONE.
OMANAH! CAN SUCH A HERO TRULY EXIST?
IMAGINE THE DANGER IF THE COMMONERS START TO QUESTION OUR ACTIONS! IT UPSETS THE ORDER OF SOCIETY!
I HEAR THAT MORE AND MORE MEN ARE JOINING THE HWAL BIN DANG.
IF THEY RAISE THE TAXES ANY HIGHER, I MAY JOIN MYSELF!

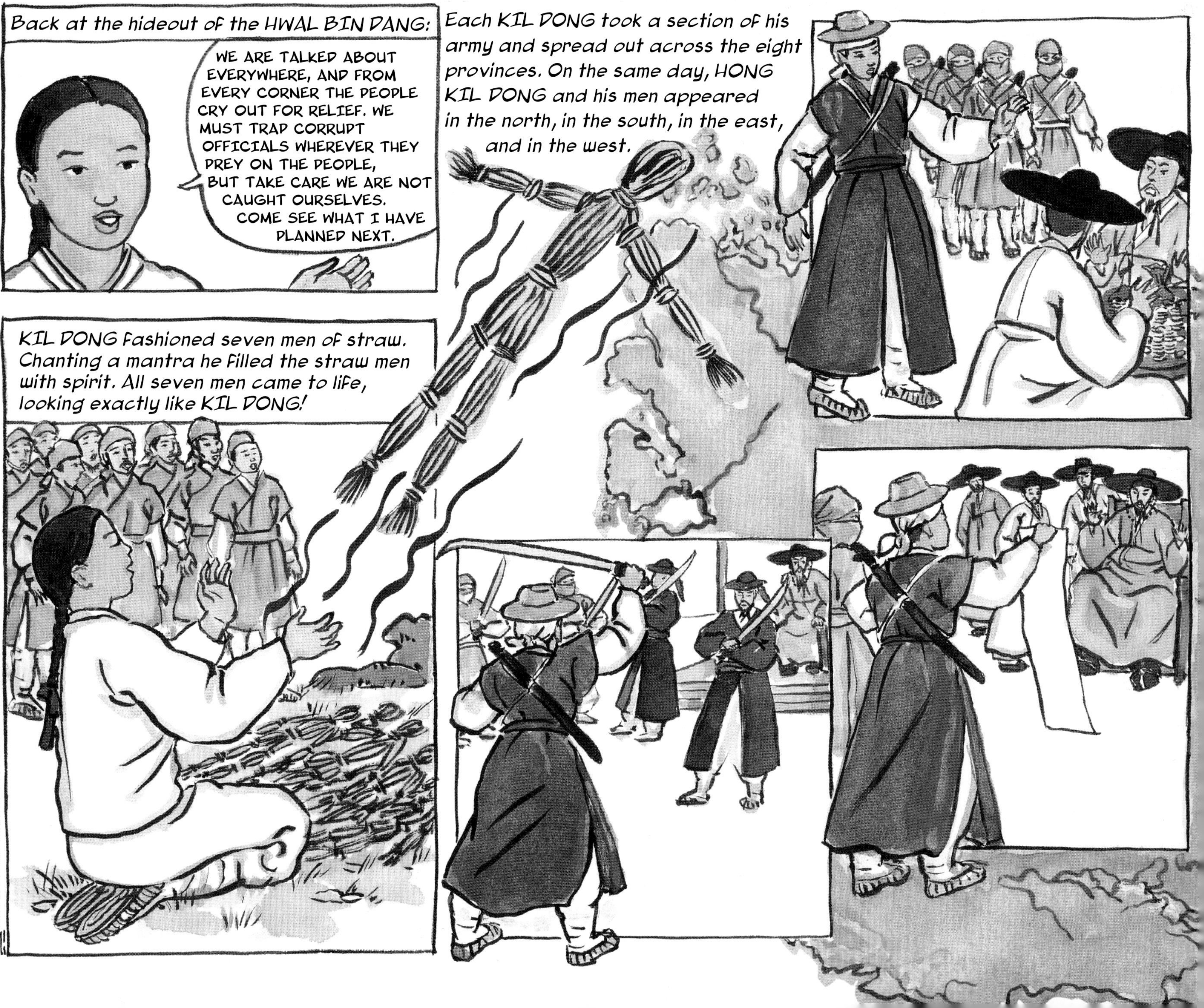
Back at the hideout of the HWAL BIN DANG:
WE ARE TALKED ABOUT EVERYWHERE, AND FROM EVERY CORNER THE PEOPLE CRY OUT FOR RELIEF. WE MUST TRAP CORRUPT OFFICIALS WHEREVER THEY PREY ON THE PEOPLE, BUT TAKE CARE WE ARE NOT CAUGHT OURSELVES. COME SEE WHAT I HAVE PLANNED NEXT.
KIL DONG fashioned seven men of straw. Chanting a mantra he filled the straw men with spirit. All seven men came to life, looking exactly like KIL DONG!
Each KIL DONG took a section of his army and spread out across the eight provinces. On the same day, HONG KIL DONG and his men appeared in the north, in the south, in the east, and in the west.

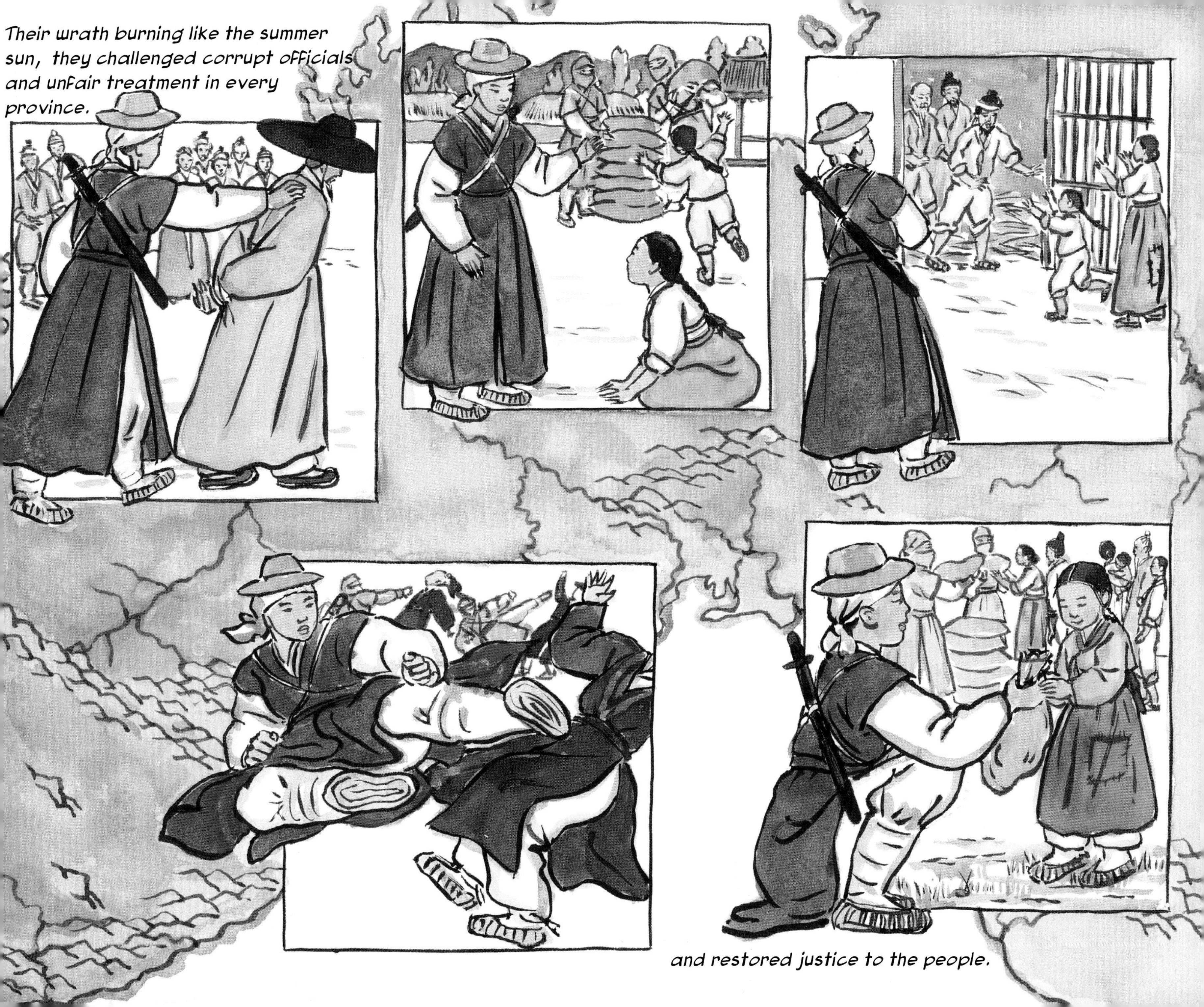
Their wrath burning like the summer sun, they challenged corrupt officials and unfair treatment in every province.
and restored justice to the people.

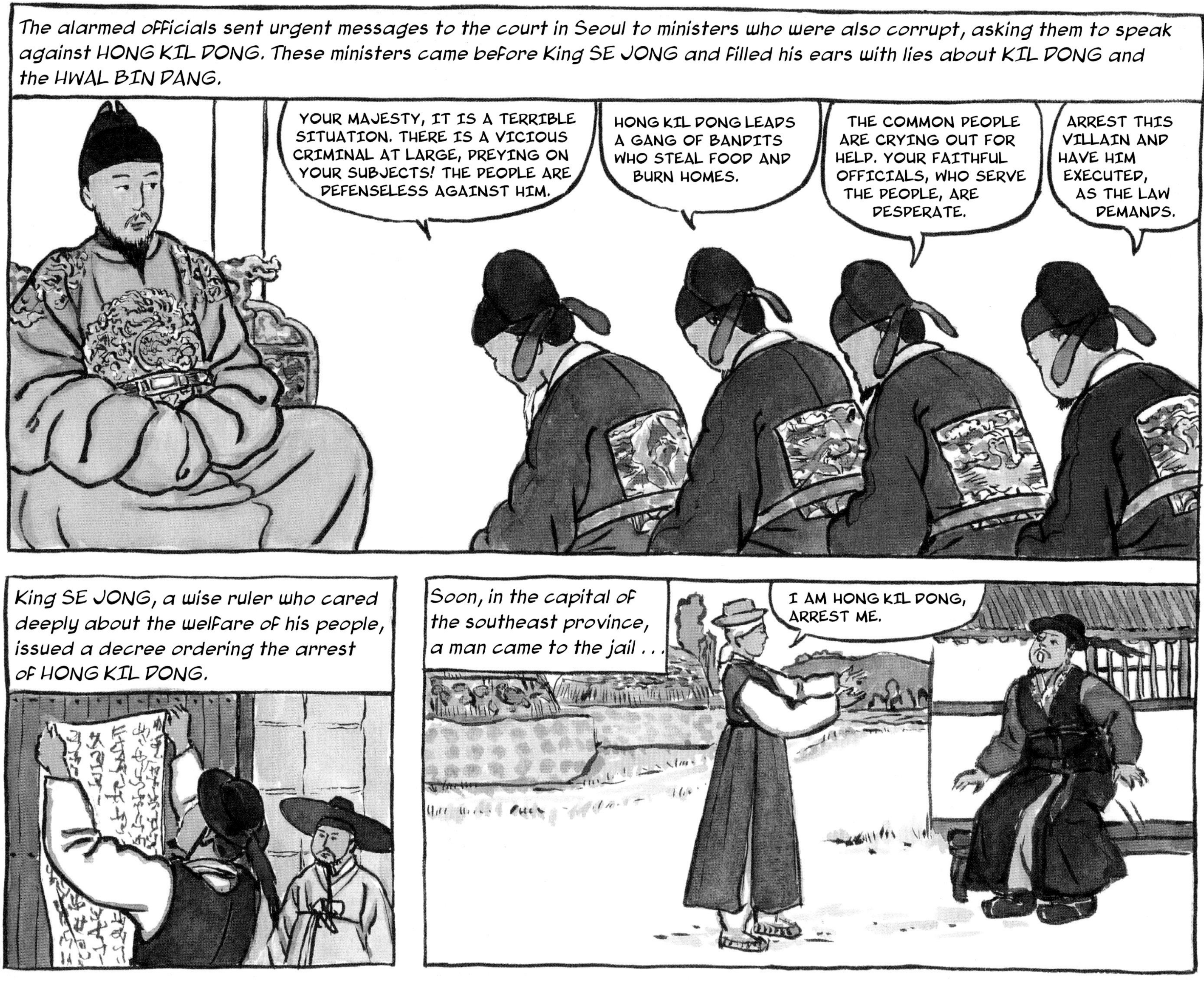
The alarmed officials sent urgent messages to the court in Seoul to ministers who were also corrupt, asking them to speak against HONG KIL DONG. These ministers came before King SE JONG and filled his ears with lies about KIL DONG and the HWAL BIN DANG.
YOUR MAJESTY, IT IS A TERRIBLE SITUATION. THERE IS A VICIOUS CRIMINAL AT LARGE, PREYING ON YOUR SUBJECTS! THE PEOPLE ARE DEFENSELESS AGAINST HIM.
HONG KIL DONG LEADS A GANG OF BANDITS WHO STEAL FOOD AND BURN HOMES.
THE COMMON PEOPLE ARE CRYING OUT FOR HELP. YOUR FAITHFUL OFFICIALS, WHO SERVE THE PEOPLE, ARE DESPERATE.
ARREST THIS VILLAIN AND HAVE HIM EXECUTED, AS THE LAW DEMANDS.
King SE JONG, a wise ruler who cared deeply about the welfare of his people, issued a decree ordering the arrest of HONG KIL DONG.
Soon, in the capital of the southeast province, a man came to the jail . . .
I AM HONG KIL DONG, ARREST ME.

FOLLOWING/PURSUIT: ADAPT TO PREVAILING CIRCUMSTANCES

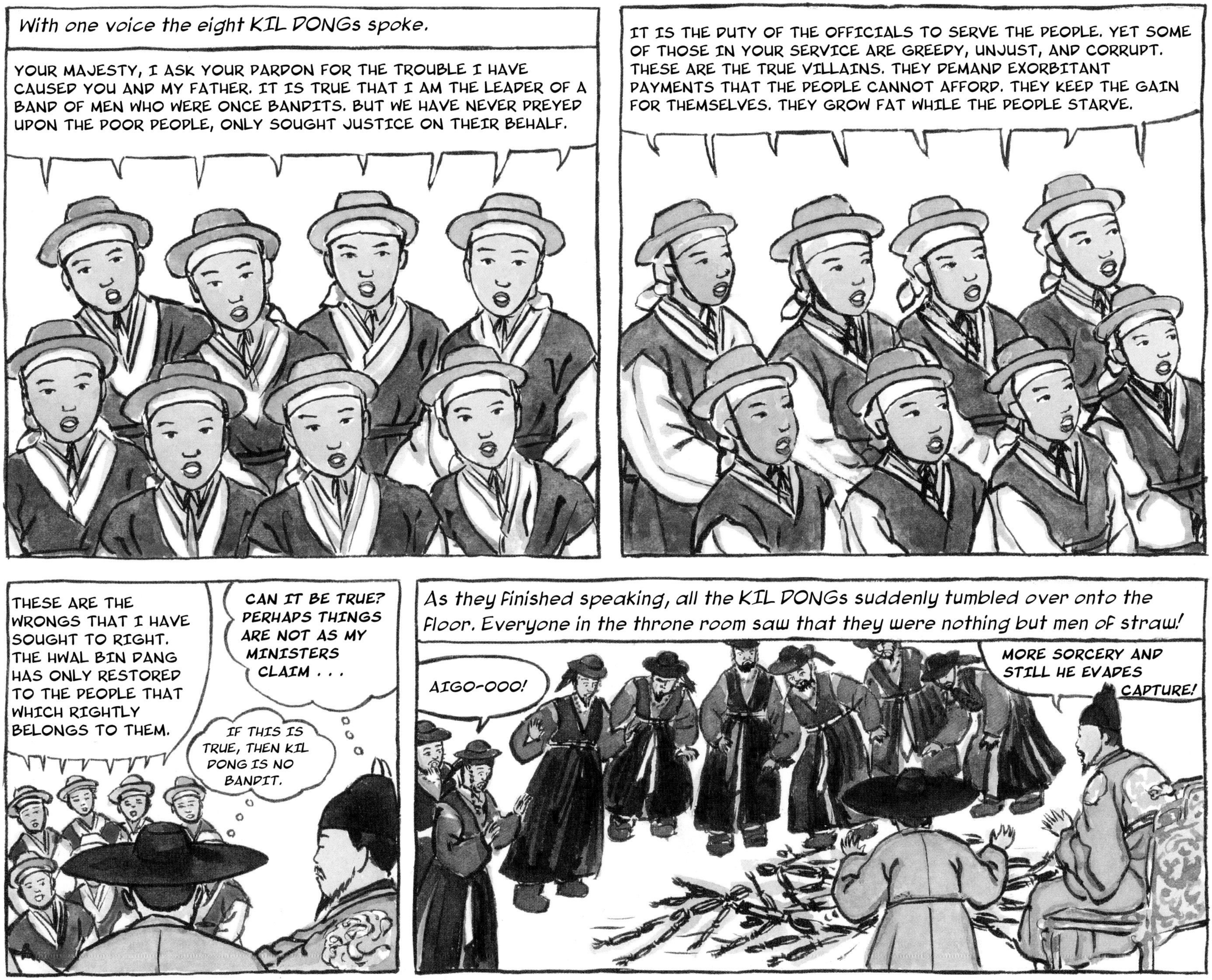

With one voice the eight KIL DONGs spoke.
YOUR MAJESTY, I ASK YOUR PARDON FOR THE TROUBLE I HAVE CAUSED YOU AND MY FATHER. IT IS TRUE THAT I AM THE LEADER OF A BAND OF MEN WHO WERE ONCE BANDITS. BUT WE HAVE NEVER PREYED UPON THE POOR PEOPLE, ONLY SOUGHT JUSTICE ON THEIR BEHALF.
IT IS THE DUTY OF THE OFFICIALS TO SERVE THE PEOPLE. YET SOME OF THOSE IN YOUR SERVICE ARE GREEDY, UNJUST, AND CORRUPT. THESE ARE THE TRUE VILLAINS. THEY DEMAND EXORBITANT PAYMENTS THAT THE PEOPLE CANNOT AFFORD. THEY KEEP THE GAIN FOR THEMSELVES. THEY GROW FAT WHILE THE PEOPLE STARVE.
THESE ARE THE WRONGS THAT I HAVE SOUGHT TO RIGHT. THE HWAL BIN DANG HAS ONLY RESTORED TO THE PEOPLE THAT WHICH RIGHTLY BELONGS TO THEM.
CAN IT BE TRUE? PERHAPS THINGS ARE NOT AS MY MINISTERS CLAIM . . .
IF THIS IS TRUE, THEN KIL DONG IS NO BANDIT.
As they finished speaking, all the KIL DONGs suddenly tumbled over onto the floor. Everyone in the throne room saw that they were nothing but men of straw!
AIGO-OOO!
MORE SORCERY AND STILL HE EVADES CAPTURE!

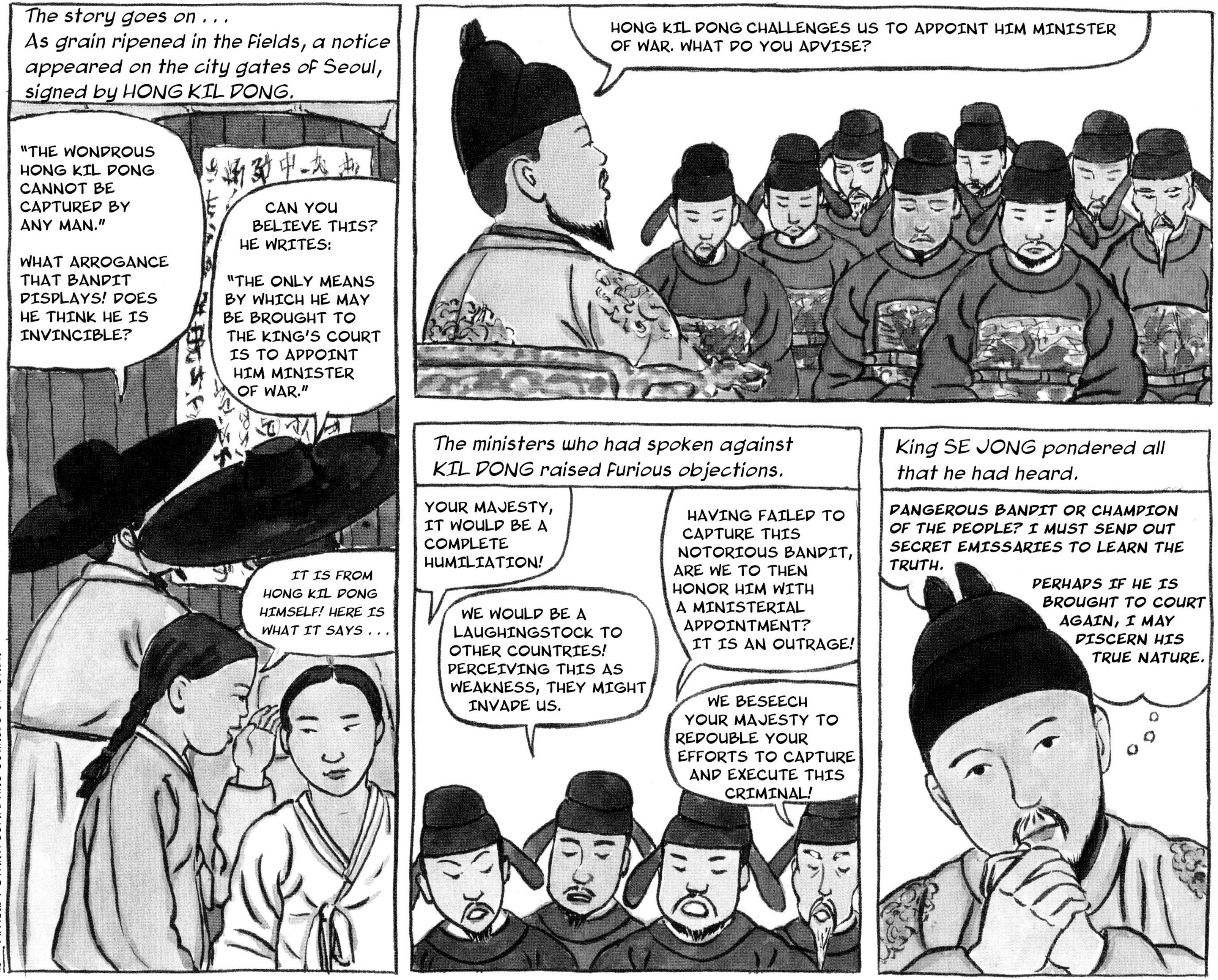

The story goes on . . .
As grain ripened in the fields, a notice appeared on the city gates of Seoul, signed by HONG KIL DONG.
"THE WONDROUS HONG KIL DONG CANNOT BE CAPTURED BY ANY MAN."
WHAT ARROGANCE THAT BANDIT DISPLAYS! DOES HE THINK HE IS INVINCIBLE?
CAN YOU BELIEVE THIS? HE WRITES:
"THE ONLY MEANS BY WHICH HE MAY BE BROUGHT TO THE KING'S COURT IS TO APPOINT HIM MINISTER OF WAR."
IT IS FROM HONG KIL DONG HIMSELF! HERE IS WHAT IT SAYS . . .
HONG KIL DONG CHALLENGES US TO APPOINT HIM MINISTER OF WAR. WHAT DO YOU ADVISE?
The ministers who had spoken against KIL DONG raised furious objections.
YOUR MAJESTY, IT WOULD BE A COMPLETE HUMILIATION!
WE WOULD BE A LAUGHINGSTOCK TO OTHER COUNTRIES! PERCEIVING THIS AS WEAKNESS, THEY MIGHT INVADE US.
HAVING FAILED TO CAPTURE THIS NOTORIOUS BANDIT, ARE WE TO THEN HONOR HIM WITH A MINISTERIAL APPOINTMENT? IT IS AN OUTRAGE!
WE BESEECH YOUR MAJESTY TO REDOUBLE YOUR EFFORTS TO CAPTURE AND EXECUTE THIS CRIMINAL!
King SE JONG pondered all that he had heard.
DANGEROUS BANDIT OR CHAMPION OF THE PEOPLE? I MUST SEND OUT SECRET EMISSARIES TO LEARN THE TRUTH.
PERHAPS IF HE IS BROUGHT TO COURT AGAIN, I MAY DISCERN HIS TRUE NATURE.

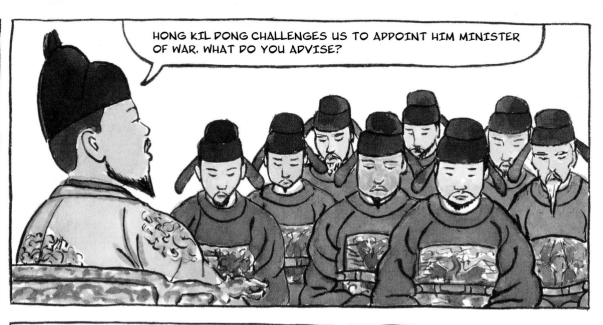

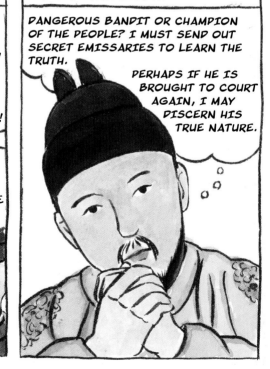

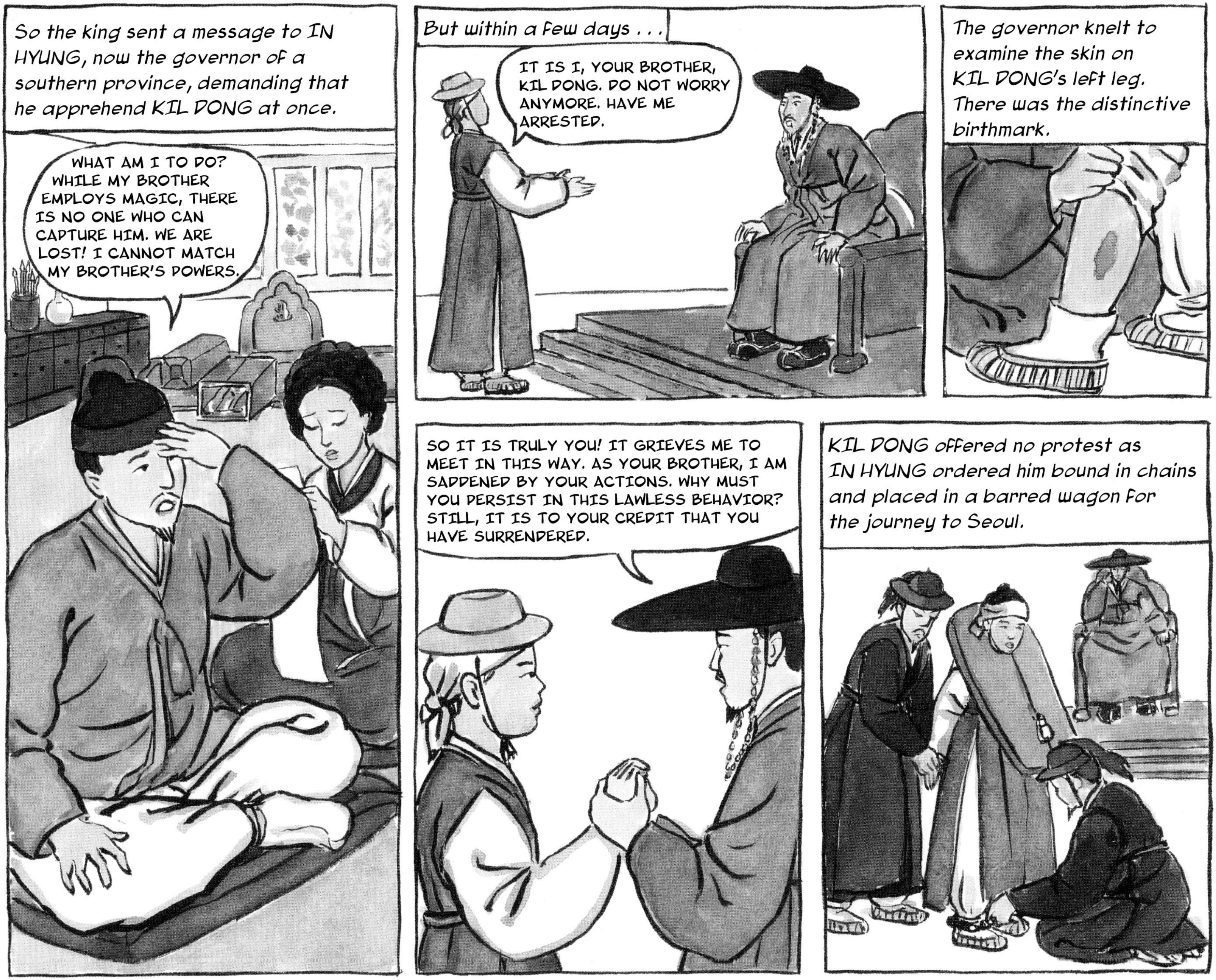
So the king sent a message to IN HYUNG, now the governor of a southern province, demanding that he apprehend KIL DONG at once.
WHAT AM I TO DO? WHILE MY BROTHER EMPLOYS MAGIC, THERE IS NO ONE WHO CAN CAPTURE HIM. WE ARE LOST! I CANNOT MATCH MY BROTHER'S POWERS.
But within a few days . . .
IT IS I, YOUR BROTHER, KIL DONG. DO NOT WORRY ANYMORE. HAVE ME ARRESTED.
The governor knelt to examine the skin on KIL DONG's left leg. There was the distinctive birthmark.
SO IT IS TRULY YOU! IT GRIEVES ME TO MEET IN THIS WAY. AS YOUR BROTHER, I AM SADDENED BY YOUR ACTIONS. WHY MUST YOU PERSIST IN THIS LAWLESS BEHAVIOR? STILL, IT IS TO YOUR CREDIT THAT YOU HAVE SURRENDERED.
KIL DONG offered no protest as IN HYUNG ordered him bound in chains and placed in a barred wagon for the journey to Seoul.

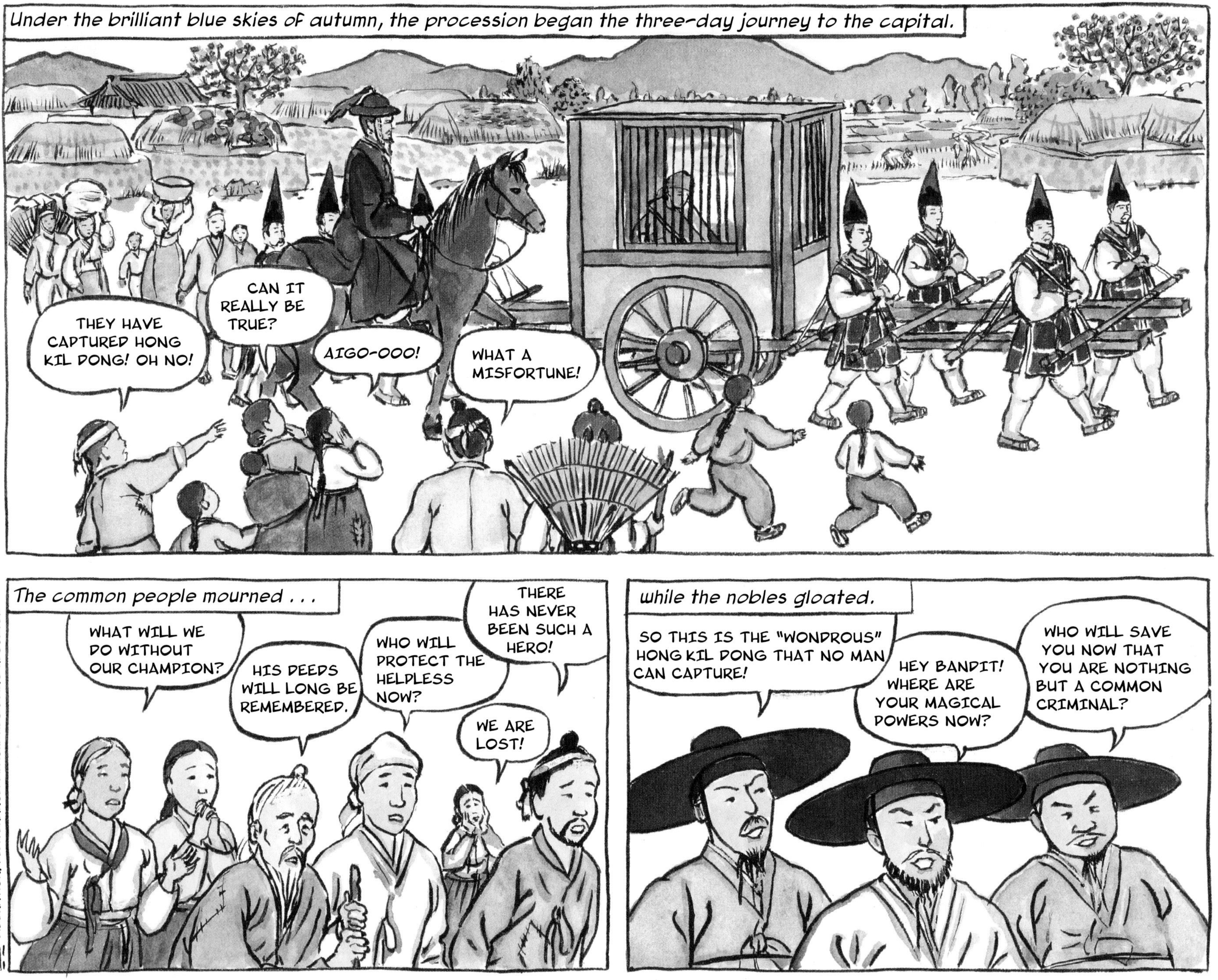
Under the brilliant blue skies of autumn, the procession began the three-day journey to the capital.
THEY HAVE CAPTURED HONG KIL DONG! OH NO!
CAN IT REALLY BE TRUE?
AIGO-OOO!
WHAT A MISFORTUNE!
The common people mourned . . .
WHAT WILL WE DO WITHOUT OUR CHAMPION?
HIS DEEDS WILL LONG BE REMEMBERED.
WHO WILL PROTECT THE HELPLESS NOW?
THERE HAS NEVER BEEN SUCH A HERO!
WE ARE LOST!
while the nobles gloated.
SO THIS IS THE "WONDROUS" HONG KIL DONG THAT NO MAN CAN CAPTURE!
HEY BANDIT! WHERE ARE YOUR MAGICAL POWERS NOW?
WHO WILL SAVE YOU NOW THAT YOU ARE NOTHING BUT A COMMON CRIMINAL?

LIBERATION/DELIVERANCE: DIFFICULTIES BEING RESOLVED

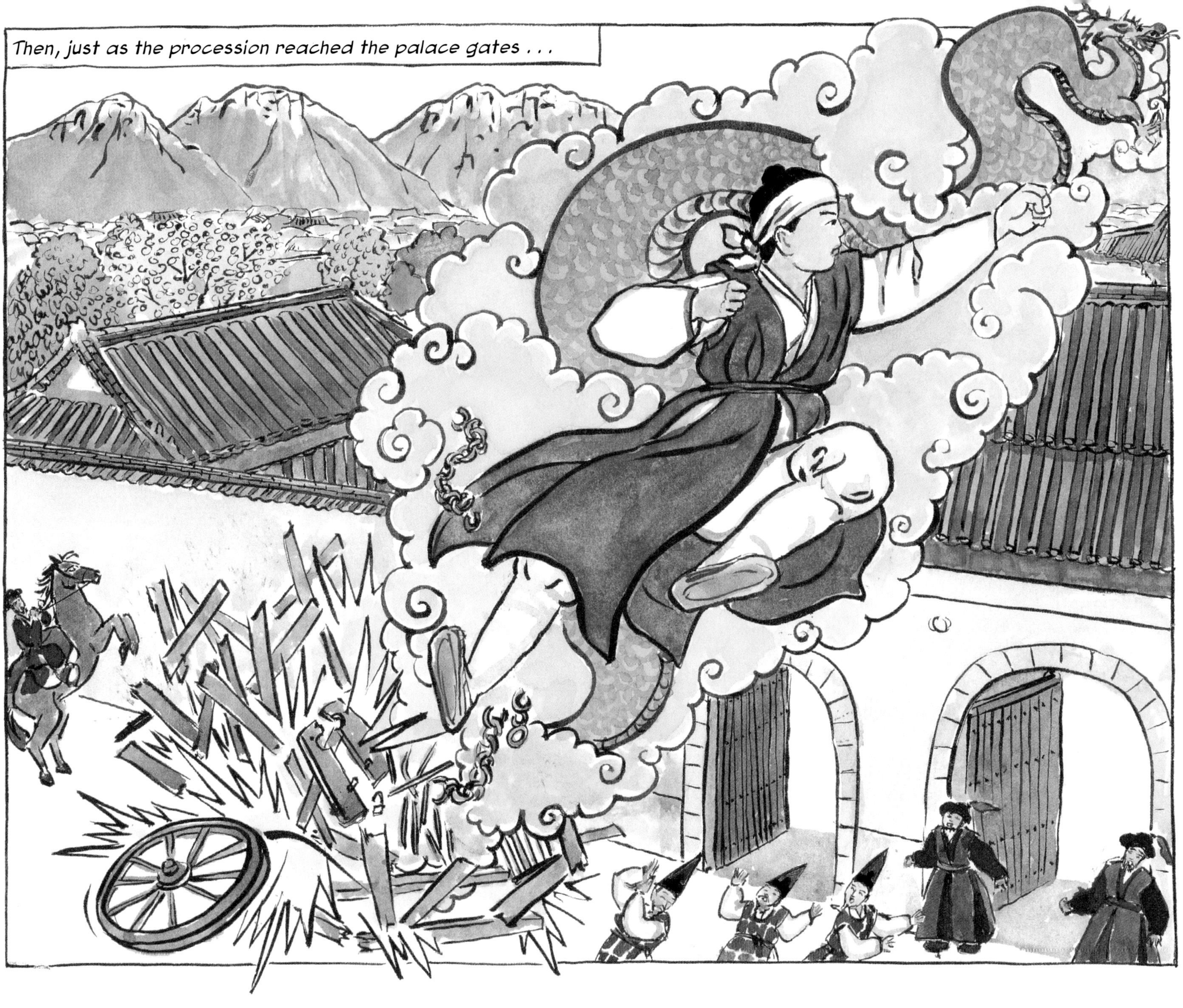
Then, just as the procession reached the palace gates . . .

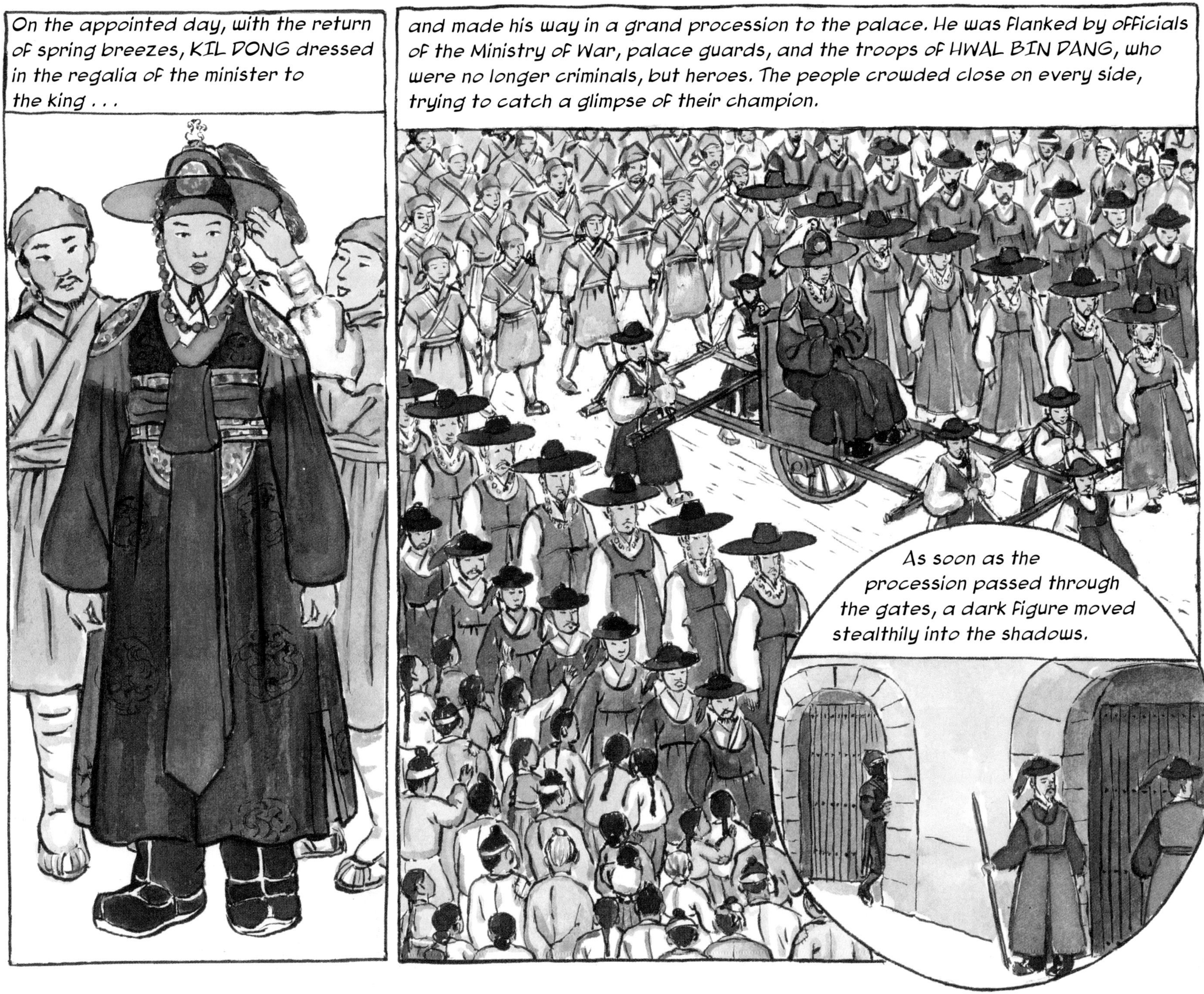
On the appointed day, with the return of spring breezes, KIL DONG dressed in the regalia of the minister to the king . . .
and made his way in a grand procession to the palace. He was flanked by officials of the Ministry of War, palace guards, and the troops of HWAL BIN DANG, who were no longer criminals, but heroes. The people crowded close on every side, trying to catch a glimpse of their champion.
As soon as the procession passed through the gates, a dark figure moved stealthily into the shadows.

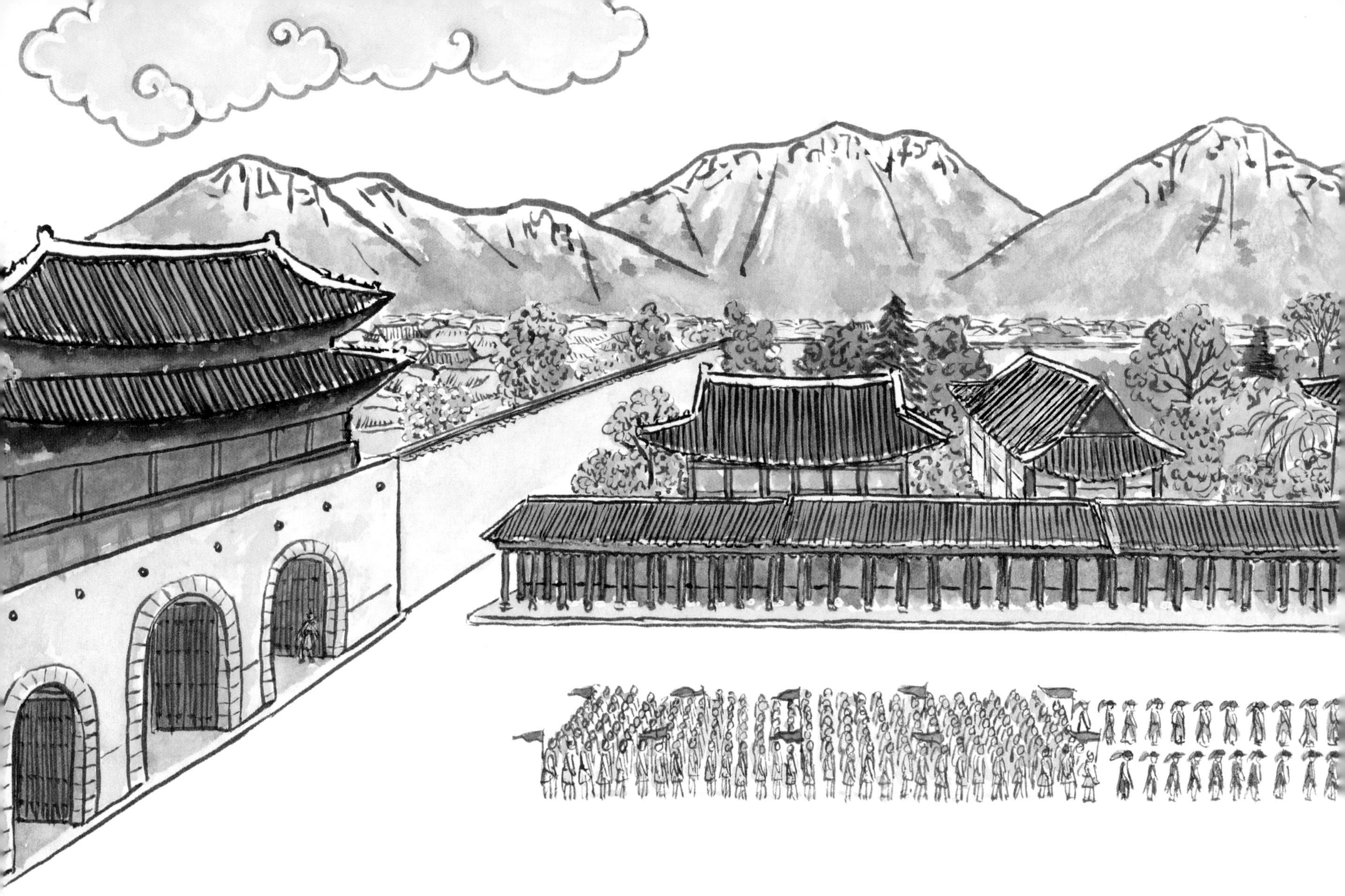

HOLDING TOGETHER:
MAN OF GREAT SPIRIT
BRINGING UNION

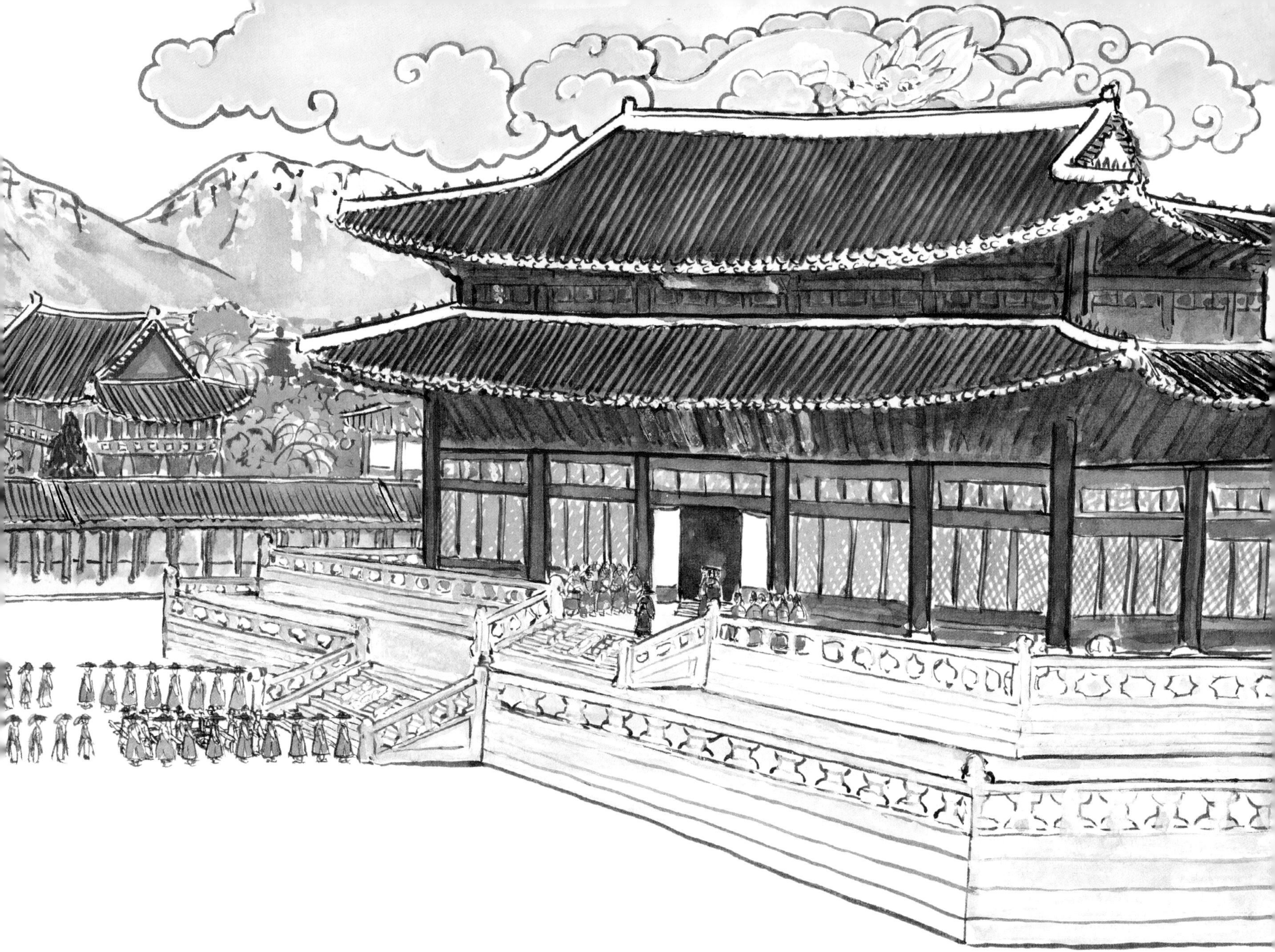

The king told KIL DONG of his dreams for improving the lives of his people.

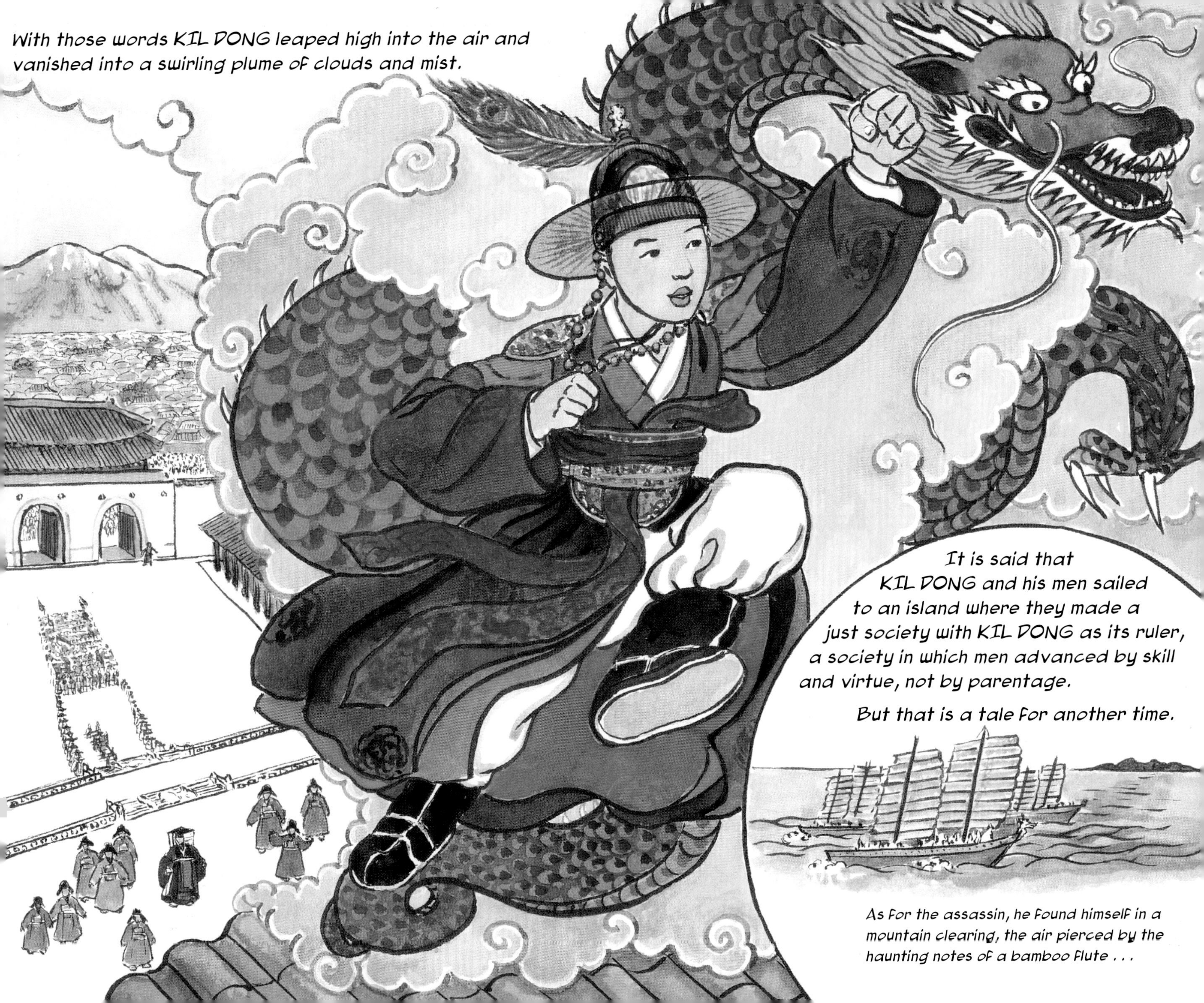
With those words KIL DONG leaped high into the air and vanished into a swirling plume of clouds and mist.
It is said that KIL DONG and his men sailed to an island where they made a just society with KIL DONG as its ruler, a society in which men advanced by skill and virtue, not by parentage.
But that is a tale for another time.
As for the assassin, he found himself in a mountain clearing, the air pierced by the haunting notes of a bamboo flute . . .

## Notes from the Author-Illustrator

I was born in 1952—the year of the dragon.

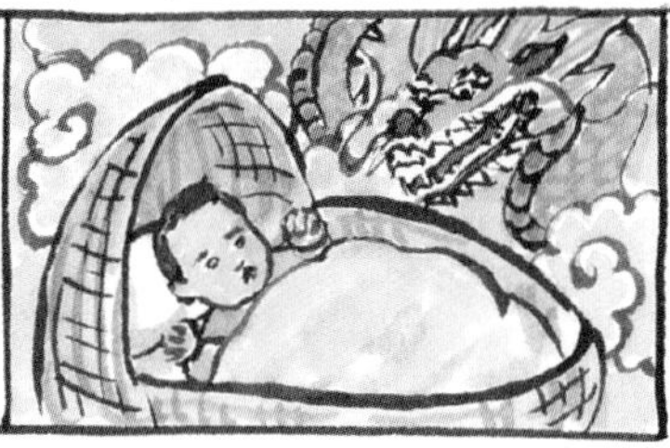

In March 1960 our family moved to Seoul, Korea, where my parents were assigned as medical missionaries. I was seven years old.

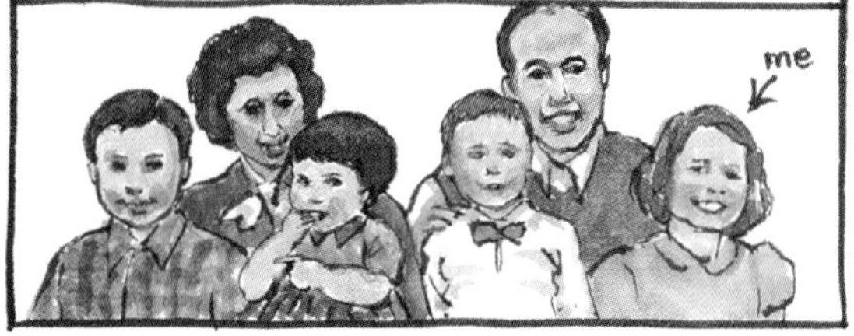
me

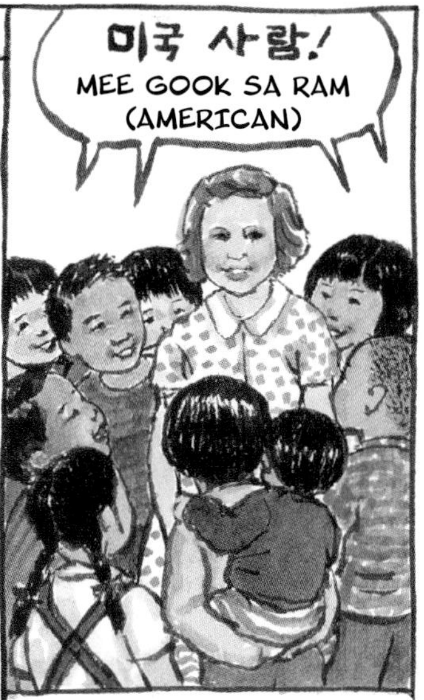
미국 사람!
MEE GOOK SA RAM
(AMERICAN)

In Korea, I really stood out.

But as I learned the language and culture, Korea quickly became my second home. Though modernization was coming fast, traditional Korean life could still be experienced in country villages.

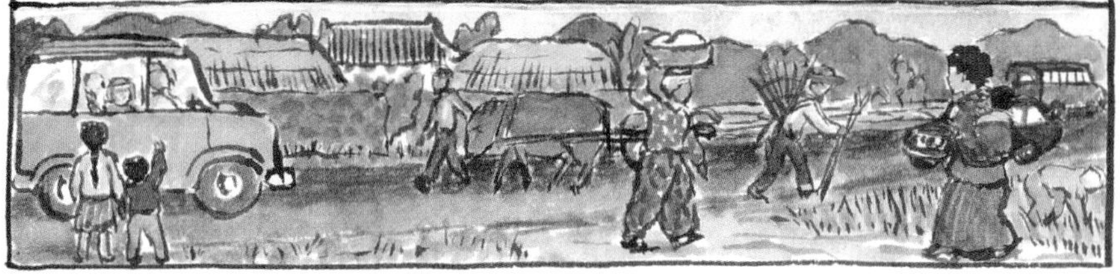

I returned to the United States for college, but spent my junior year back in Korea at Ewha Woman's University. One of the subjects I studied was Korean painting.

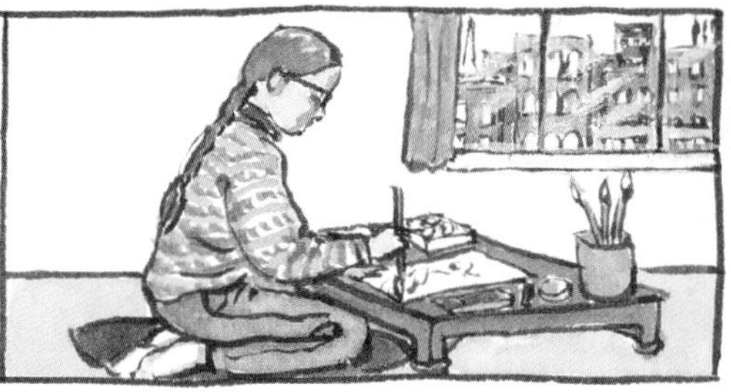

Back in the States, I finished college and began a career writing and illustrating children's books. Over the years I sometimes looked for book ideas in the Korean tales I had heard growing up. I was familiar with the well-known story of the boy hero HONG KIL DONG. One day, while I was doing research at the Harvard-Yenching library at Harvard University, I came upon the novel THE TALE OF HONG KIL DONG, as written by HO KYUN in the seventeenth century, in a book of Korean literature that had been translated into English.

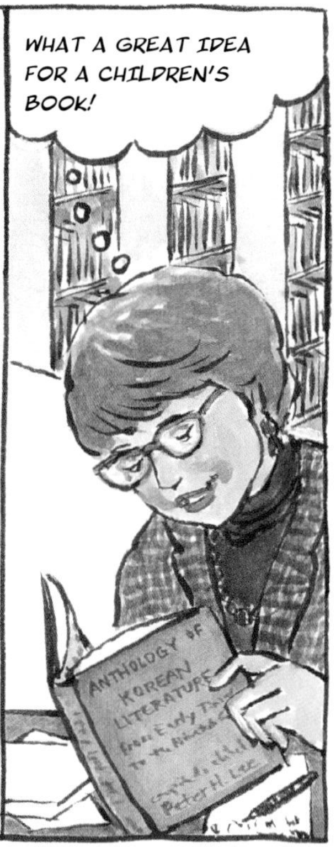
WHAT A GREAT IDEA FOR A CHILDREN'S BOOK!
ANTHOLOGY OF KOREAN LITERATURE

HO KYUN (pronounced huh kyoon) lived from 1569 to 1618 and was the son of yangban parents. His father was a minister, and HO KYUN also served in a government post. But he sympathized with the plight of those who were barred from social advancement because one parent was a commoner. Though fictional, THE TALE OF HONG KIL DONG was said to be inspired by the exploits of justice-seeking outlaws, both historical figures and characters in Chinese literature. It was a reaction against the strict rules of the Confucian society that divided people by social class. These rules determined who would have the chance to learn to read and write. HO KYUN was executed for his alleged association with a group of illegitimate sons who attempted to overthrow the government.

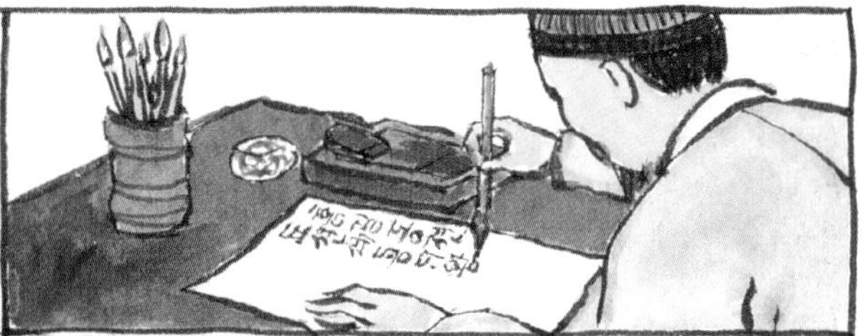

THE TALE OF HONG KIL DONG (Hong Kil Dong Jun) was written about the same time that the Spanish writer Cervantes wrote DON QUIXOTE. HO KYUN chose to write his story not in the Chinese characters that were traditionally used for literature, but in HAN GUL, the Korean alphabet that had been created 150 years earlier. The novel, possibly the first written in Korean, could easily be read by Koreans of all classes. HO KYUN also decided to set the story during the reign of the historical king SE JONG. I love the circle that is made by the first book written using the Korean alphabet having as a character the very king who gave his people that alphabet.

THE I CHING OR BOOK OF CHANGES IS AN ANCIENT CHINESE DIVINATION MANUAL AND BOOK OF WISDOM. ONE OF THE "FIVE CLASSICS" OR FUNDAMENTAL BOOKS OF CONFUCIANISM, ITS POETIC TEXT, AND UNCANNY EFFECTIVENESS IN FORETELLING THE FUTURE HAVE MADE IT A POPULAR SPIRITUAL RESOURCE.

The historical King SE JONG was one of the greatest rulers of Korea's CHOSUN dynasty (also called the YI dynasty). His reign (1419-1450) was a golden age of culture and reform, marked by efforts to better the lives of Korea's people. He passed laws to make taxes fair, so that people only paid what they could afford. He formed a group of scholars, the Hall for the Assembly of the Wise, and supported their studies and research. This resulted in many discoveries, inventions, and advancements, including a sundial, a water clock, and maps of the solar system. He invested in the development of printing, revolutionizing Korea's system of movable metal type, which had been invented in 1403. Many books were produced, including textbooks about how to farm and medical books on treating illness. SE JONG is most notable for instructing a group of scholars to develop an alphabet for the Korean language. Previously, Korean was solely a spoken language, and all writing was done in Chinese characters. King SE JONG's alphabet made it possible for all his people to read and write in their own language.

## NOTES ON SPELLING, PRONUNCIATION, AND MEANINGS OF SOME KOREAN WORDS:

When Korean writing is reproduced in English, different spellings may be used for the same sounds. So, HONG KIL DONG may also be written as HONG GIL-DONG or as HONG KIL-TONG.

The vowels in Korean words used in this book are pronounced as follows:
A as in father in the words HWAL BIN DANG and YANGBAN
E as in set in SE JONG
I as in ill in KIL DONG
O as in oh in HONG KIL DONG
U as in fuss in IN HYUNG
The sound of R in CHO RAN is rolled, as in Spanish.

OMANAH and AIGO are exclamations of surprise, like "oh!"
YANGBAN describes someone of the upper social class, someone nobly born.

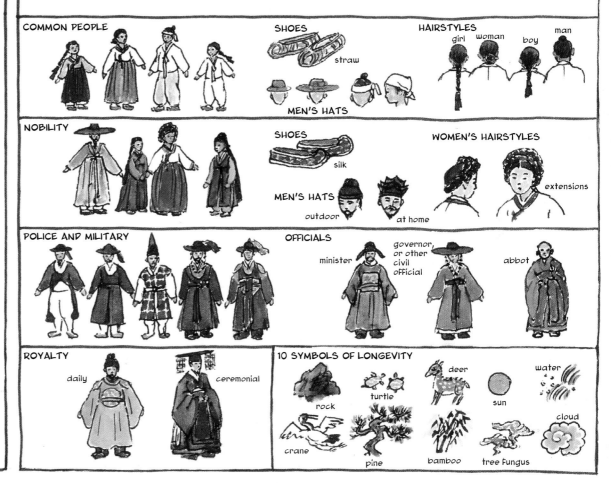

COMMON PEOPLE

SHOES — straw

MEN'S HATS

HAIRSTYLES — girl, woman, boy, man

NOBILITY

SHOES — silk

MEN'S HATS — outdoor, at home

WOMEN'S HAIRSTYLES — extensions

POLICE AND MILITARY

OFFICIALS — minister, governor, or other civil official, abbot

ROYALTY — daily, ceremonial

10 SYMBOLS OF LONGEVITY — rock, turtle, deer, sun, water, crane, pine, bamboo, tree fungus, cloud

# 대단히 감사합니다!

With deep thanks to those who gave me
invaluable assistance with references,
information, inspiration, and encouragement:

CHOONG NAM YOON, Librarian, and HYANG KOOK
 LEE, Library Assistant, the Korean collection,
 Harvard-Yenching Library, Harvard University
SOUNG-HWAON KIM of the Kyonggi Provincial
 Museum, Korea
DAVID MCCANN, Korea Foundation Professor of
 Korean Literature, Harvard University;
BRUCE FULTON, Young-Bin Min Professor of
 Korean Literature and Literary Translation,
 Department of Asian Studies, University of
 British Columbia
WON BAE and IP BOON PARK
CHON YE TAYLOR and JEONG KYO YOON
PHOEBE YEH and JUDY O'MALLEY
SUSAN SHERMAN and DENNIS O'REILLY

And to my family for all their love and
support, with particular thanks to Yunhee,
O. B., and Perry.

FOR TAZ

## Sources

The English version of the tale that I found at the
Harvard-Yenching Library is The Tale of Hong Kil Tong,
translated by Marshall Pihl, in Peter Lee's 1981
Anthology of Korean Literature: From Early Times to the
Nineteenth Century (Honolulu: University of Hawaii, 1981).

I also used a Korean text with English footnotes found in
Korean Literary Reader with a Short History of Korean
Literature by Doo Soo Suh (Seoul: Dong-A Publishing,
1965).

My primary source for clothing references was Kwon
Oh-Chang's beautiful book, Korean Costumes During the
Chosun Dynasty (Seoul: Hyunam Publishing, 1998).

A chapter on Ho Kyun in Kim Kichung's An Introduction
to Classical Korean Literature: From Hyangga to
P'ansori (Armonk, N.Y.: M. E. Sharpe, 1996, pp. 141–157)
gave me important insights into the author's character
and concerns.

All of these sources, and many others I found useful,
are available at the Harvard-Yenching Library,
Harvard University.

PUBLISHED BY CHARLESBRIDGE
85 MAIN STREET
WATERTOWN, MA 02472
(617) 926-0329
WWW.CHARLESBRIDGE.COM

LIBRARY OF CONGRESS CATALOGING-IN-PUBLICATION DATA

O'BRIEN, ANNE SIBLEY.
  THE LEGEND OF HONG KIL DONG, THE ROBIN HOOD OF KOREA / ANNE SIBLEY O'BRIEN.
    P. CM.
  BASED ON A CLASSIC TALE FROM EARLY 17TH CENTURY KOREA.
INCLUDES BIBLIOGRAPHICAL REFERENCES.

ISBN-13: 978-1-58089-302-2 (REINFORCED FOR LIBRARY USE)
ISBN-10: 1-58089-302-3 (REINFORCED FOR LIBRARY USE)

1. GRAPHIC NOVELS. I. TITLE.
PN6727.027T36 2006
741.5--DC22                        2005056941

PRINTED IN SINGAPORE

(HC) 10 9 8 7 6 5 4 3 2 1

ILLUSTRATIONS DONE IN INK AND WATERCOLOR ON ARCHES PAPER
DISPLAY TYPE SET IN LINOTYPE'S VISIGOTH
TEXT TYPE SET IN BLAMBOT COMICS FONTS, DESIGNED BY NATE PIEKOS
COLOR SEPARATIONS BY CHROMA GRAPHICS, SINGAPORE
PRINTED AND BOUND BY IMAGO, SINGAPORE
PRODUCTION SUPERVISION BY BRIAN G. WALKER
DESIGNED BY SUSAN MALLORY SHERMAN

THE PAGES OF HONG KIL DONG ON THE ENDLEAVES ARE A FACSIMILE REPRODUCTION
OF AN ARCHAIC KOREAN WOODBLOCK EDITION.

나도 [illegible]

여간쳥ᄒᆞ시니 부인이 옷슬 떨치고 밧그로 나가시니 승상이

무류ᄒᆞ신 ᄎᆞᆷ의 부인의 도도ᄒᆞ고 집을 이달나 무슈히 ᄎᆞ탄

ᄒᆞ시고 외당으로 나오시니 마ᄎᆞᆷ 시비 춘섬이 상을 드리거ᄂᆞᆯ

좌우 고요ᄒᆞᆷ을 인ᄒᆞ여 춘섬을 잇글고 원앙지낙을 일의

시니 져근 울화을 더르시나 심니의 못니 한탄ᄒᆞ시더라 춘

섬이 비록 쳔인이나 저덕이 순직ᄒᆞᆫ지라 불의예 승상의 위엄

으로 친근ᄒᆞ시니 간이 위령치 못ᄒᆞ여 슌종ᄒᆞᆫ 후로난 그날붓

텨 즁문 밧긔 나지 아니ᄒᆞ고 ᄒᆡᆼ실을 닥그ᄂᆡ 답 못텨 그ᄋᆡ

쳐신ᄉᆡᆨ이 당ᄒᆞ미 가쳐ᄒᆞᄂᆞᆫ 방의 오ᄉᆡᆨ운무 영농ᄒᆞ며 향ᄂᆡ 그치

ᄒᆞ더니 춘미ᄒᆞᆷ의 ᄒᆞᆫᄐᆡᄒᆞ니 일ᄀᆡ 그 남ᄌᆞ리 ᄉᆞᆷ일 후의 승상이

드러와 보시니 일변 깃거ᄒᆞ오나 그 쳔ᄉᆡᆼ되믈 앗기시더라 일홈

을 길동이라 ᄒᆞ니라 이 아ᄒᆡ 졈〻 ᄌᆞ라미 긔골이 비상ᄒᆞ여 ᄒᆞᆫ

말을 드르면 열 말을 알고 ᄒᆞᆫ 번 보면 모로거시 업더라 일〻

은 승상이 길동을 다리고 ᄂᆡ당의 드러가 부인을 ᄃᆡᄒᆞ야 탄식

왈 이 아ᄒᆡ 비록 영웅이오나 쳔ᄉᆡᆼ이라 무엇의 쓰리요 원통할ᄉᆞ

부인의 고집이여 ᄎᆞ회 막급이로소이다 부인이 그 연고을 뭇ᄌᆞ

오니 승상이 양미을 빈츅ᄒᆞ여 왈 부인이 젼일의 ᄂᆡ 말을 드르

시던들 이 아ᄒᆡ 부인 복즁의 낫슬 다 엇저 쳔ᄉᆡᆼ이 되리요 인

ᄒᆞ여 몽ᄉᆞ 열셜화ᄒᆞ시니 부인이 츄연 왈 ᄎᆞ역 쳔슈오니 엇

지 실력으로 ᄒᆞ오리ᄭᆞ 셰월이 여류ᄒᆞ야 길동의 나히 팔셰라 상

하 다 아니 층찬ᄒᆞ리 업고 ᄃᆡ감도 ᄉᆞ랑ᄒᆞ시나 길동은 가ᄉᆞᆷ의

원한이 부친을 부친이라 못ᄒᆞ고 형을 형이라 부르지 못ᄒᆞ